T0328873

The girls of Hillcrest High . . .

Suzanne—When will she learn that no one is safe from the pain of betrayal?

Nikki—Can she learn to trust her best friend or her boyfriend again?

Katia—Will super-jock John Badillo ever think of her as more than Keith's little sister?

Victoria—Will her carefree life shatter as she learns just how dangerous secrets can be?

#1 Most Likely to Deceive

#2 Just Like Sisters

Jennifer Baker

AN ARCHWAY PAPERBACK
Published by POCKET BOOKS
New York London Toronto Sydney Tokyo Singapore

AN ARCHWAY PAPERBACK *Original*

An Archway Paperback published by
POCKET BOOKS, a division of Simon & Schuster Inc.
1230 Avenue of the Americas, New York, NY 10020

Produced by Daniel Weiss Associates, Inc., New York

ISBN: 978-1-4814-2876-7

First Archway Paperback printing November 1995

10 9 8 7 6 5 4 3 2 1

Printed in the U.S.A.

IL 7+

One

"Do the words *complete and utter fraud* mean anything to you?" Victoria Hill shifted the black cordless phone to her right ear and put a diamond earring in her left. Nothing fancy, just plain diamond studs—after all, it was only a Sunday morning, and she was alone in her bedroom at home. She didn't need to impress anyone—yet. But as she caught a glimpse of herself in the full-length mirror, wearing white silk pajamas under a red satin robe, she knew she looked fantastic, even if her wavy red hair was a little sleep-rumpled.

Victoria waited a moment for a reply from the other end, but there was only silence, so she continued. "How about *liar, impostor, charlatan—*"

"What are you talking about?" Nikki Stewart,

Victoria's best friend, finally responded. She sounded groggy.

"I said, do the words *complete and utter fraud* mean anything to you?" Victoria couldn't wait to tell Nikki what she had discovered about the new girl in town, Suzanne Willis. She wouldn't have admitted it, but she was secretly jealous of the friendship that had been building between Nikki and Suzanne. Nikki was *her* best friend, and she hated the way Suzanne had just nosed her way in.

Just wait till Nikki finds out that Suzanne was lying to her all along, Victoria thought, and smiled in anticipation.

"Victoria, it's too early in the morning to play guessing games," Nikki said. Victoria heard a loud yawn.

"Did I wake you up?" Victoria asked. "What's the matter—did you and Luke stay out late last night?"

Nikki had been dating her boyfriend, Luke, for about two years. They were practically the most solid couple at Hillcrest High.

"No," Nikki said, sounding angry. "You didn't wake me. Actually, I couldn't sleep last night. I got bored tossing and turning in bed, so I moved onto the couch."

"Are you sick or something?" Victoria asked, suddenly concerned.

"More like depressed," Nikki replied.

Nikki Stewart—depressed? Victoria found that hard to believe. Nikki almost never got bummed, about anything. She was the most positive person Victoria knew. "You probably just need some caffeine," Victoria told her best friend. "Nikki, wake up, smell the coffee, make yourself a cup of cappuccino, but do something! I've only got the juiciest piece of gossip to hit Hillcrest this millennium," she announced, propping herself on the end of her bed. "It's incredibly good, and it's incredibly hot. I bet nobody knows anything about this, but you can be the first—no, make that the second—to know."

"If it's all the same to you, I'm not in the mood for any gossip," Nikki replied.

"*What?* Are you kidding me? Since when are you not interested in hearing gossip?" Victoria asked.

"Since last night," Nikki said, sounding even more dejected. "In fact, I think I'm about to be the topic of some incredibly hot gossip myself."

"Come on, what could anyone possibly have to say about *you?*" Victoria asked. Nikki was only the most popular, well-liked student at Hillcrest High. Everyone adored her, from the jocks to the smart kids to the teachers to . . . infinity. "If anyone's saying anything, it's probably a compliment. Some girl is probably sitting around with her friends right now, talking about how she wishes she were you."

"Not today she doesn't," Nikki grumbled.

"Nik? You're serious, aren't you?" Victoria was starting to worry. "What's up?"

"I don't want to talk about it," Nikki said. "Not over the phone, anyway."

"Well, then we've both got news too hot to discuss over the phone. I'll be right over," Victoria said. "As soon as I get dressed. Okay?"

"Victoria, I don't know if I feel like—"

"Nik, whatever's happened, we'll deal with it. Together," Victoria said. "Talking always helps. Don't worry, okay? I'll be over in half an hour." She clicked the off button and set the phone down on her bedside table. She was a little disappointed she had to wait to tell Nikki all about Suzanne's secret, but it would be better to tell her in person. That way Victoria could see Nikki's face when she told her that the girl she'd taken under her wing had betrayed her.

On her way to the closet to pick out an outfit to wear, Victoria stepped over the previous day's clothes. In all the excitement about sharing her hot gossip with Nikki, she had almost forgotten her horrible date the night before.

Victoria had gone over to Ian Houghton's the previous evening. He was gorgeous and practically the only cute guy left at Hillcrest she hadn't already dated and dumped. She had dressed to kill, but Ian hadn't seemed to notice. All he'd wanted to do on their date was send messages back and forth to his cyber-friends in an Internet club.

He'd ignored Victoria. Completely.

Victoria took a sip of cappuccino from the oversized green cup on her desk.

"How could he even look at a computer monitor when I was around?" Victoria said out loud as she walked into her closet and started rummaging through a stack of sweat-shirts.

At least the night hadn't been a total loss. On her way out she'd eavesdropped on an intimate conversation between Ian's father and Suzanne's mother, who had just returned from a dinner date. Valerie Willis had confided in Bob Houghton that Suzanne's father hadn't died, as she'd told her daughter. She had lied to Suzanne about her father to protect her from the truth: that they'd had an affair, and before she knew it, she was pregnant and he was gone.

Victoria still couldn't believe it. Little Miss Instant Popularity had told everyone a sob story about her father having been killed in an accident before she was born. But the real truth was that he had just skipped out. This had to be the biggest secret in all of Hillcrest!

Victoria couldn't wait to tell Nikki. Maybe then Nikki would have second thoughts about her new best friend. Maybe she'd start to see that the Willises weren't what they pretended to be.

Of course, Victoria had been suspicious of the Willises from the start. It didn't make sense: one day Suzanne and her mother were living in an apartment in Brooklyn with Suzanne's grandparents, and the next Valerie Willis was opening a posh exercise studio in Hillcrest.

Well, I know something Suzanne doesn't know, Victoria thought with a smile as she tossed some clothes behind her onto the bed. Something that could turn her perfect new life upside down.

Victoria quickly dressed, pulling on black leggings and an old sweatshirt, then went downstairs to the kitchen to put her empty coffee cup in the sink. She wiped her hands on a towel hanging on the refrigerator next to the hook where she kept her car keys.

"Where are you going, Victoria?" Mr. Hill asked as she hurried past her father. He was sitting at the table, sipping from his coffee mug.

She walked toward the door that led to the garage, not bothering to answer him. By the way her father had slurred the end of her name, Victoria could tell he'd already been drinking.

"See you, Daddy," was all she said. And before her father could say another word or, worse, give her a good-morning kiss that reeked of alcohol, she was out the door. She rushed to her car in the driveway. The sooner she got away from her father, the better.

Besides, she couldn't wait another minute to tell Nikki all about Suzanne's secret. Once Nikki knew the real Suzanne, Victoria would be back to being *her* best friend—the way things should have been all along.

I hate this feeling! Nikki Stewart thought as she frowned, drumming her fingers against the arm of the overstuffed couch. I can't believe Luke and Suzanne. Thanks to them, I'm totally depressed.

She rested her chin on her arm, and her long blond hair dangled over the couch arm, practically reaching the floor. Not that Nikki didn't have her problems, but most often they came down to one thing: her parents. They worked constantly, fought just as often, and ignored her. But she usually managed to focus on what was right in her life.

Nikki stared blankly out the living room window, her head pounding with an angry headache. It was a late-September morning.

The sky was a clear, deep blue. Red and yellow leaves occasionally fluttered to the ground, and the scent from the nearby apple orchard wafted through the open window. Normally Nikki would have been in a terrific mood, getting ready for a fun Sunday afternoon of shopping or working out. Or spending some time with her boyfriend, Luke Martinson. Ex-boyfriend is more like it, she thought.

Nikki couldn't stop thinking about what had happened the night before, and about Luke's pathetic apology afterward. She pressed her hands over her eyes, trying to blot out the image of Luke and Suzanne that had been haunting her ever since she'd caught the two of them making out on the golf course.

She'd been looking for Luke because she'd missed him . . . and maybe also because she was feeling a little guilty after going bowling with Keith Stein.

Keith was one of Luke's best friends. And Nikki had known Keith practically forever. He'd always been her pal, too.

But the previous night something totally different and unexpected had happened between them. They'd been having a blast bowling when she suddenly found herself in Keith's arms. Then she'd thought about Luke and stopped herself from going further. Or had Keith been the one to pull away? Either way, there was no denying that Keith had an effect on her. But none of that mattered now. The important thing was that nothing had happened between them—nothing like what she had seen happening between Luke and Suzanne.

The worst part was that it had taken the sight of Luke kissing another girl to make her realize she was still totally in love with him. Lately Nikki had been feeling that she and Luke were growing apart. They were definitely not communicating very well, that was for sure, and Luke had been even more glum than usual.

Nikki knew she could have been more sympathetic. Luke did have a tough home life, and he was always busy working at the Tunesmith, a popular music store in Hillcrest. But she was getting pretty tired of cutting him slack, tired of his never-ending bad moods. She wanted to have fun, not mope around all the time with a brooding kind of guy.

But Luke wasn't depressed when I saw him at the golf course last night, Nikki reminded herself painfully. In fact, he looked incredibly happy with his arms around Suzanne, his lips pressed against hers . . .

Nikki hugged her pillow sadly. She had spent more than a few evenings with Luke in that exact same spot, talking and kissing and looking up at the stars. Tears stung her eyes. She had thought Suzanne was her friend. Now she felt totally betrayed.

Nikki grabbed a tissue and dabbed her eyes as she recalled Luke racing after her, trying to explain. Well, that was one apology she wasn't about to accept.

"C'mon, Nikki, just give me a chance to explain," he'd said.

"I don't want to hear anything you have to say. Leave me alone, Luke. Just get out of my way," Nikki had yelled, running away as fast as she could.

She wondered now if Luke had gone back to Suzanne afterward. Had they continued with their little picnic, feeding each other grapes in between kisses?

She shuddered. It was too disgusting to think about. Then she'd had to listen to Luke's pathetic apology over the phone later. And Suzanne had already called twice that morning. Nikki hadn't taken her calls, though. She wished she'd never have to see or speak to either one of them ever again. The only problem was, they'd both be at school on Monday.

"Great. Just great," she muttered, wondering when Victoria would show up. Usually she would look forward to spending a Sunday morning with Victoria, rehashing their Saturday-night dates, swapping clothes, or giving each other makeovers. But that day she wasn't sure she wanted to tell Victoria what had happened—it was too humiliating. Victoria was the one who'd been saying all along not to trust Suzanne. She wouldn't be at all surprised to hear what had happened—she seemed to have been expecting it ever since Suzanne moved to Hillcrest a few weeks earlier. Nikki could already hear her friend saying, "I told you so."

No, she didn't want to discuss it: her new friend and her boyfriend, together. *Really* together.

Another tear trickled down Nikki's cheek, and she quickly brushed it away. She'd cried enough. She didn't deserve to be unhappy. She didn't deserve any of this!

If only I could go back to last night and start over, she thought. She wouldn't let Luke and Suzanne get together in the first place. She wouldn't let Luke out of her sight. I should have known, she told herself.

She didn't care if Suzanne called a hundred times, or if Luke crawled across broken glass to apologize. She was through with both of them. For good.

Two

Suzanne walked her mountain bike the last few yards up Nikki's long gravel driveway. Her heart was pounding, but it wasn't from the three-mile ride over to the Stewarts' house in the ritzy Hillcrest Hollow section of town. She was nervous about seeing Nikki. She had no idea how Nikki was going to react to what she had to say. But Suzanne had never avoided a confrontation before, and she wasn't going to start now.

She was halfway to the Stewarts' huge house when a vintage silver BMW sports car pulled into the driveway. "Oh, no," Suzanne muttered.

Victoria stepped out of her car and slammed the door behind her. "Well, if it isn't Suzanne Willis," she said. Her wavy red hair glinted in the bright sun as she walked toward Suzanne. "What a coincidence. I was just thinking about you."

"Hi, Victoria," Suzanne said, trying to sound cheerful even though Victoria was the last person in the world she wanted to see at that moment. Suzanne didn't have anything against Victoria—she was Nikki's friend and one of the coolest people at school. Even now, though she was only wearing black leggings and an oversized, well-worn red sweatshirt, Victoria still managed to look terrific. It was just that Suzanne had hoped to have some time alone with Nikki. To explain about the previous night.

Suzanne wondered if Victoria knew about her and Luke. If she did, she would only make things more difficult for Suzanne. Suzanne knew that Victoria had taken an instant dislike to her the moment they met. Now that Suzanne was in trouble with Nikki, Victoria would delight in complicating matters even further.

"What's up?" Suzanne asked, trying to sound casual. She fluffed out her dark hair self-consciously. It was a little damp with sweat, but otherwise she figured she looked presentable. She was wearing bike shorts and a baby T-shirt.

"Oh . . . not much." Victoria joined Suzanne

on the porch outside the front door. "So, what are *you* doing here?"

Suzanne rang the doorbell. "I have something to talk about with Nikki. It's kind of personal, actually."

"Well, anything you can say to Nikki, you can say to me," Victoria said. "*We* don't keep any secrets from each other."

What's that supposed to mean? Suzanne wondered as the door swung open. Nikki was standing there, still in her pajamas even though it was almost noon. Her blond hair was all rumpled, and there were dark circles under her eyes. She was holding a tissue in her hand, and she looked as if she'd been crying.

"Hi," Nikki said. She gave Victoria a weak smile, but she didn't even look at Suzanne.

She knows. She saw everything. And she hates me, Suzanne thought. "Hi, Nikki," she said as cheerfully as she could. "Can I come in?"

"Actually, I'd rather you didn't," Nikki said in an icy tone.

Victoria's jaw dropped open. She stared at Nikki, then at Suzanne. "What's going on here? Did I miss something?"

"Please, Nikki—please, let me in. I can explain," Suzanne begged. "Just give me a chance."

"Explain *what?*" Victoria asked, leaning

closer to Suzanne. She seemed desperate to find out what was going on.

"There's nothing to explain," Nikki said. "I saw you. I wish I hadn't, but I did."

"What are you guys talking about? Is this why you're so upset?" Victoria asked Nikki.

Suzanne bit her lip. So far, things were going even worse than she'd imagined. "Nikki, I'm sorry if you're feeling upset—"

Nikki glared at Suzanne. "I'm not just upset. I'm angry. No, make that furious—at *you!*"

Suzanne felt as if she'd just been punched in the stomach, but she wasn't about to give up. "Nikki, please . . ."

"Maybe you should give her a chance," Victoria said to Nikki.

Suzanne stared at Victoria suspiciously. Since when was Victoria on her side—in anything?

"Why should I?" Nikki asked Victoria.

"Just let her in. The three of us need to talk," Victoria said. "Besides, I have something very important to say to both of you."

"Well . . ." Nikki hesitated.

"Trust me," Victoria said, brushing past Nikki into the house as if she owned it.

Nikki shrugged and stepped aside to let Suzanne by. "You can come in, I guess."

Maybe Nikki was going to give her another

chance after all, Suzanne thought hopefully as they passed the large, sunken living room and headed upstairs to Nikki's bedroom. "Maybe you and I should talk first . . . in private," Suzanne suggested, nodding in Victoria's direction.

"Anything you have to say to me, Victoria can hear," Nikki said coldly.

"That's what I told her," Victoria said, dropping into a huge pink chair in Nikki's room. "So, you go first, and then I'll say what I have to say afterward. What is it?" She looked pointedly at Suzanne.

Nikki sat at the end of her bed, pushing aside a large teddy bear. Suzanne was too nervous to sit. She paced back and forth in front of the two of them. Why did Victoria have to be there? She wasn't going to be able to explain everything with Victoria pouncing on her every word.

"Go ahead," Victoria prompted.

"Nikki, I'm so sorry—" Suzanne began.

"Sorry for what?" Victoria interrupted, her green eyes narrowing at Suzanne. "What happened?"

"I never meant to hurt you," Suzanne went on, ignoring Victoria. "I've never done anything like that before."

"Why should I care whether you've done this before? It only matters that you did it now," Nikki replied.

"Will somebody *please* tell me what this is all about?" Victoria insisted.

Suzanne glanced nervously at Nikki. She wished Victoria would just disappear.

"I saw Luke and Suzanne together last night," Nikki said slowly. "You know he and I haven't been getting along that well lately. So last night I went bowling with Keith. But then I realized I should just go talk to Luke, work things out. Only when I found him at the golf course . . ." She paused, unable to go on.

"I was there," Suzanne finished for her.

"You weren't just there," Nikki said angrily. "You guys were kissing, and I don't know what else would have happened if Luke hadn't seen me when he did."

"Nothing else would have happened," Suzanne said. "Nikki, I didn't mean to kiss him, I—"

"I don't believe this!" Victoria cried. "You and Luke? How could you do something like that? How could you even think about doing something like that?"

"I know," Suzanne said. "I feel terrible. I never should have been with Luke last night. But I ran into him downtown," she explained. "It wasn't planned or anything. We just started talking, and we were both feeling kind of blue, so we decided—"

"So you decided you'd kiss him and try to

cheer both of you up?" Victoria shook her head. "You're unbelievable, you know that? Since when is it *your* job to cheer up *Nikki's* boyfriend? They were doing just fine before *you* came to town."

"Look, it's not exactly a secret that things haven't been going well between you two," Suzanne said to Nikki, once again trying to ignore Victoria.

Victoria walked over to the bed and put her arms around Nikki. "I tried to warn you about her."

Nikki shrugged out of Victoria's grasp. "I really don't need you telling me 'I told you so' right now."

"Don't get mad at me," Victoria said. *"I'm* not the one who tried to steal your boyfriend."

"I wasn't trying to steal Luke," Suzanne insisted. "I really thought from what you guys both said that maybe you were breaking up."

"I won't deny we're going through a rough time, but that doesn't mean I want to break up with him," Nikki said roughly.

"Nikki, I'm so sorry," Suzanne said again. She didn't know what else she could say. With Victoria in the room, criticizing every word she said, Suzanne felt she wasn't getting anywhere. The more she tried to explain, the more unforgivable kissing Luke seemed.

Suzanne knew what she had done with

Luke was wrong, but despite her apology to Nikki, she didn't totally regret kissing him. She was attracted to Luke, he was attracted to her . . . it hadn't been just an empty kiss. They had real feelings for each other. At least Suzanne knew she did for Luke. And Luke had said he felt the same way about her. Part of her wished that Nikki hadn't found them when she did. Maybe if she and Luke had spent the rest of the evening together uninterrupted, they might have solidified their relationship.

But she wasn't going to tell Nikki any of that. Luke had made it clear whom he wanted to be with when he raced after Nikki that night. No, there was no hope for her and Luke. The most she could do now was salvage her friendship with Nikki. And that was unlikely with Victoria in the room.

She took a deep breath. "I know there's nothing I can do to make up for what I did, Nikki. But please believe me, I never meant for any of this to happen, and it won't happen again. I hope you can forgive me, and—"

"Nikki, if I were you, I wouldn't forgive her," Victoria interrupted. "And I wouldn't believe a word she says, either. She's been lying about things since the day we met her. She's a liar—just like her mother." Victoria stared at Suzanne, a challenging look in her eyes.

"My mother? What does my mother have to do with anything?" Suzanne asked, totally confused.

Victoria smiled. "She told everyone that your father's dead."

"Yes. Because he *is* dead." Suzanne felt her heart beating faster. What was Victoria getting at?

Victoria shrugged. "That's not what your mother told Ian's dad. I was over at Ian's house last night, and I happened to overhear the real story."

"The *real* story?" Suzanne asked. "What's that?" The last thing she wanted to deal with were Victoria's lies.

"That your father abandoned your mother when she was pregnant with you," Victoria said. "He didn't die. He just didn't want anything to do with you and your mother, that's all."

Suzanne put her hand on Nikki's desk to steady herself. "B-but . . . that can't be true," she sputtered.

"Victoria, you're not making this up, are you?" Nikki asked.

"The only person who's been making things up is Valerie Willis," Victoria said. "And since she's been lying to her own daughter since the day she was born, it wouldn't surprise me if Suzanne turned out to be a liar, too."

"I don't understand. Why are you saying this? Why would you want to hurt me this way?"

"Listen, Suzanne, I'm just repeating what I heard. I think you're asking the wrong person all these questions. Obviously you need to have a little chat with your dear old mom," Victoria said.

"I—I have to go," Suzanne said, her eyes brimming with tears, then ran out of Nikki's room and down the hallway. She didn't want to hear another word from Victoria. Was her father really alive? Why had her mother lied to her? Or was Victoria the one who was lying?

She didn't know what to think, but if Victoria was telling the truth and her father really was alive, she wanted to hear it from her mother. She couldn't believe she would have lied to her her whole life. She thought they were close. She thought her mother told her everything. How could she do something like that? Now both Victoria and Ian's father knew more about her own life than Suzanne did.

And suppose her father really was alive . . . Where was he? *Who* was he? Why had he walked out on them?

Suzanne's head was spinning with questions as she got onto her bicycle. Before she did anything else, she needed to talk to her mother. She needed to know the truth.

Three

Keith Stein stretched his arms over his head and yawned. He pulled up the shade on the window beside his bed and immediately covered his eyes with his hand, shielding them from the bright morning light. It had been a late night . . . a very late night. He hadn't gotten home until after three. And if it hadn't been for the stack of ten-dollar bills sitting on top of his desk, he wouldn't have believed Saturday night had even happened. First bowling with Nikki . . . then almost kissing her . . . then telling her to go back to Luke. And then the card game.

It had started out so innocently. Just another Saturday night in Hillcrest. He and Nikki had gone bowling after football practice.

Alone.

Keith had been into Nikki for a long time,

but Luke was one of his best friends. He'd never made a play for Nikki, even though he'd been dying to. He'd always sworn by his loyalty to Luke, and he'd planned to stick to it . . . until the previous night at the bowling alley. Just as things had seemed as though they might have gotten hot and heavy, he'd pulled back. Keith hadn't been able to go through with it.

Why do I have to be so loyal? he thought now, reaching for the stack of money on his desk. *I'm not doing myself any favors.*

If he were more like John Badillo, his other buddy, he would have been all over Nikki in a second. John had a well-deserved reputation as a love-'em-and-leave-'em kind of guy. Girls were attracted to his tall, dark, and handsome looks, and the fact that he was Hillcrest's star quarterback didn't hurt, either.

Lately John had been checking out Keith's little sister, Katia. Keith told himself he was going to have to keep an eye on that situation. He didn't want Katia's heart broken by John, no matter how much she said she liked him.

Keith riffled the stack of bills. He couldn't believe how much money he was holding in his hands. Recently he'd started playing small-stakes poker with his friends. Then Sally Ross had introduced him to her father's poker game. The men had looked strangely at Keith when he'd bought into that first game. But not only had Keith proven he belonged in their league, he'd shown them he was the king of it!

Maybe a few of his winning hands the night before could be attributed to pure luck. But nobody could stay that lucky all night. That was when he'd known it wasn't luck. He was good. Really good.

And the more games he played, the more money he was going to have. Now all he had to do was decide what to do with it. He'd been wanting a motorcycle for a long time. If he kept winning, he'd have enough money to buy one outright, paid for in full with cold cash.

What do you mean, *if* you keep winning? *When* you keep winning is more like it, Keith thought with a smile.

"I don't want to tell anyone . . . not yet," Katia Stein said to John Badillo while they ate lunch together on Sunday at Katia's house. They'd just gotten back from a trip downtown to the Tunesmith to pick up some new tapes to listen to in John's car. The rest of Katia's family was out, and they had the house to themselves.

"Why not?" John asked. "I think everyone should know about us. I *want* everyone to know." He reached across the butcher-block table and put his hand over hers.

Katia smiled as she looked into John's dark

brown eyes. She loved the feel of his strong hand on hers. And part of her couldn't wait for everyone to find out about them, either—but another part of her was enjoying keeping it a secret. Especially from her big brother, Keith, who kept insisting John was only hanging around Katia because of him. But after their romantic dinner date the night before at the Arboretum, it was obvious: Katia and John were officially a couple. An item. Together.

"We can tell everyone soon, maybe at school tomorrow. But I'd like to have today to ourselves." She squeezed John's hand.

"Sounds good to me," John said.

Katia smiled. She didn't know why it had taken so long for her and John to get together. She'd had a crush on him practically since she was born—okay, maybe only since the year before, officially. But back then she'd been a nobody freshman, and John was a popular junior. She'd known she didn't stand a chance. The fact that she had been plump and spent too much time sitting around at home munching popcorn and watching football games on the tube with Keith instead of exercising and socializing hadn't helped. But with some tips from Victoria—who'd been dating Keith at the time—she'd managed to turn her eating habits and her wardrobe around. And by the time her sophomore year started, Katia felt ready—for

John, or any other guy she was interested in.

"What about Suzanne?" she'd asked him after their first kiss the night before. They'd been sitting on the hood of John's car, watching the sun set over the lake.

"What about her?" John had asked, laughing. "We went out a few times. But it was nothing serious, trust me. It was more like a convenience thing. Then things got really rough between us. . . ."

Katia knew that John and Suzanne's brief relationship had ended after some disastrous date, but she didn't know the details. "And do you usually date girls because they're . . . convenient?" Katia had asked.

"No! Well, maybe. Sometimes in the past I might have," John had admitted. "But not you. You're different. You're the real thing."

"Really?" Katia had felt a flutter of excitement as John leaned closer.

"Yes, really," John had whispered. "C'mon, let's stop talking about other girls. Let's talk about you. About us." Then he'd put his hand on her back and kissed her again.

Nikki was lying on her bed, reading a fashion magazine, when the telephone rang. Without thinking, she grabbed the cordless phone off the nightstand. "Hello?"

"Nikki, I'm so glad you answered the

phone," Luke said. "I was afraid you'd be screening your calls, avoiding me."

"Maybe I should have been," Nikki said, frowning. She'd only answered the phone because Victoria was supposed to call about their plans to go hiking at Pequot State Park later that afternoon. "Luke, I don't want to talk to you." She wished she could get the image of Luke and Suzanne kissing out of her mind. Maybe then she could start mending her damaged relationship with her boyfriend. But not yet. The wound was still too fresh.

"We have to talk," Luke pleaded. "I'll pick you up after I get off work, okay? We can go someplace quiet, and I can explain."

"Suzanne was already over here this morning, explaining," Nikki said. "I think I've had enough explaining for one day. Besides, I have other plans for this afternoon."

"Nikki, give me a chance. I was awake the whole night, worrying about you . . . about us."

"Well, I'm *so* sorry you had insomnia, but maybe you should have thought about us before you started kissing someone else," Nikki said.

All of a sudden a vision of her and Keith at the bowling alley flashed through her mind—how she'd kissed Keith in a friendly way, and how she'd wanted to kiss him even more.

I would have kissed him again, she realized, *if he hadn't stopped me.*

But the point was, he *had* stopped her, and Suzanne hadn't stopped Luke. And from what she'd seen, Luke had been as into it as Suzanne was.

"Nik, I know it's really hard for you to believe this, but I'm not interested in Suzanne. The only girl I'm interested in is the one I've been in love with for the past two years—you."

Nikki felt her anger and her fervent resolve not to forgive Luke begin to weaken. But she couldn't let him off the hook that easily, just because he'd said something nice, something romantic. "I need some time to think about it," she said.

"But Nikki—"

"Maybe tomorrow. Bye." Nikki clicked a button on the cordless phone and cut Luke off in midsentence. She knew it was mean to hang up on him like that, but she wanted him to feel as rotten as she did.

Besides, if she'd stayed on the phone with him, she might have let on how relieved she was that there was still hope for them as a couple.

That was more hope than she had about the possibility of remaining friends with Suzanne. Victoria had been right—Suzanne was bad news.

Even as she held that thought, Nikki had an image of how hurt and surprised Suzanne had looked when Victoria sprang the secret about her father. For a split second Nikki wanted to call her and make sure she was all right. But Suzanne didn't deserve that kind of friendship, not after the way she'd acted. Suzanne would just have to deal with her own problems by herself. The same way Nikki was dealing with hers.

Four

Suzanne peered through the window in the door of the large first-floor aerobics room at Willis Workout. There was her mother, smiling and leading a step aerobics class, the way she did every Sunday at one o'clock. She looked completely relaxed and happy, as if nothing in the world were wrong.

As if she hasn't been keeping the biggest secret from me for my entire life! Suzanne thought angrily.

She yanked the door open and stormed into the workout room, her lug-soled shoes squeaking loudly on the hardwood floor.

The music playing from the large speakers on the wall was mellow, and a group of exercisers was in the middle of a series of warm-up stretches. Everyone looked up at Suzanne as she marched into the room, but she didn't care. She went right up to her mother, who was staring at her, a puzzled expression on her face.

"Mom, we need to talk. Now!" Suzanne demanded.

"Suzanne, what's going on?" Ms. Willis asked. She never stopped leading the class.

"That's what I'd like to know," Suzanne replied. "Maybe you'll finally get around to telling me, since you haven't for the past sixteen years."

Suzanne's mother finally stopped moving and stared at her. "What are you talking about?"

"I doubt you want to get into it right now, in front of everyone," Suzanne said under her breath. "Let's go into your office."

"I can't right now—I'm in the middle of a class. Just let me get through this and take a quick shower, and then we'll talk." Valerie Willis smiled at Suzanne. "Maybe over some takeout Chinese from Imperial Garden. How does that sound?"

"Mom, I don't feel like eating. This isn't girls' night out, this is serious!" Suzanne pleaded, ignoring the stares from the students around her. "I need to talk to you right now."

"Are you in some kind of trouble?" Ms. Willis asked, suddenly sounding alarmed.

"No—but *you* might be if you don't come to

your office and tell me exactly what's going on!"

Ms. Willis scanned the studio. "Gloria, would you mind taking over?" she called to a woman in the second row. "As you heard, I need to talk to my daughter—excuse me, everyone. Sorry for the interruption. I'll be back as soon as I can." She grabbed a towel from the floor and put it around her neck. "Come on, then. Let's talk."

Suzanne followed her mother out of the workout room and up the white spiral staircase to the second floor of the elaborate fitness studio, where her mother's large office was located. They went into the office, and Valerie closed the door behind them.

"I don't appreciate your barging into my workout like that," she said, her face tightening to an angry scowl. "It looks very bad to the clients."

"Really?" Suzanne said, tracing the lettering on the nameplate on her mother's desk. "Well, *I* don't appreciate being lied to. Especially by my own mother."

"Lied to?" Ms. Willis sat down in the chair behind her desk, a confused look on her face. "What do you mean? When have I lied to you?"

"How would I know?" Suzanne said. "I only find stuff out from other people because you tell the truth to everyone except me." She glared at her mother. "Do you have any idea how humiliated I feel right now? Not to mention hurt, upset, confused—"

"Suzanne, you have to tell me what this is all about," Ms. Willis said.

"Like you don't know! Mom, you can forget about playing dumb, because you're rotten at it," Suzanne yelled. "I know, okay? I heard from Victoria, and believe me, she really loved being the one who told me you've been lying to me my whole life about my father." Suzanne's voice cracked on the last word. She fought back tears as she continued, "Mom, she said *he's alive.* I hope you're going to sit there and tell me Victoria made the whole thing up, because if she didn't, if that's the truth, then I don't know what I'm going to do. I feel like I'm losing my mind." She leaned on the desk, suddenly exhausted by her emotional outburst. "So what is it, Mom? Is he dead or alive?"

Her mother looked shell-shocked. She pushed her chair away from her desk. "I guess I should have been honest with you from the start," she said quietly. "But you've got to believe me, I didn't want you to find out this way—"

"I'll bet. You didn't want me to find out, period!" Suzanne interrupted. "So he is alive, then?"

Ms. Willis nodded. "Yes." She paused. "He is."

"How could you lie about something so

important?" Suzanne asked, sinking into a chair opposite her mother. She felt as if she was about to cry, but she forced back the tears. "How could you keep something so hugely significant from me? Mom, why don't I know anything about this man? Who is he? Where is he? And did he really dump you, the way Victoria said?"

"Hold on a second. Slow down. How did Victoria find out?" Ms. Willis demanded. "And what exactly did she say?"

"She was at Ian Houghton's house last night," Suzanne explained. "And I guess you felt like Ian's dad was worth confiding in about my father, even though *I'm* not."

"It's not that I didn't want you to know about him," Ms. Willis said, standing up and moving toward Suzanne. "I just . . . Let me start at the beginning, okay? I only did what I thought was best, and given the circumstances, I think you'll understand. Maybe you'll even forgive me someday. Maybe you're old enough now to know the truth." She reached out to touch Suzanne's shoulder.

Suzanne pulled away violently. She didn't think she would ever understand being lied to by her own mother. She didn't *want* to be that understanding. After the way her mother had kept the truth from her, she didn't deserve Suzanne's understanding, much less her forgiveness.

"You remember I once told you about going to Hollywood when I was twenty to become an actress, right?" Valerie began, moving toward the couch in her office. "Well, that's true, but what I didn't tell you was that I met your father then, when I was working as a waitress, waiting for the big break that never came."

"Am I supposed to feel sorry for you now?" Suzanne scoffed, turning to face her mother. This was unbelievable!

"Suzanne, all I'm asking is that you try to imagine what it was like for me. Just put yourself in my shoes," she said calmly.

"Well, that's not possible, because I don't lie to the people I love," Suzanne said.

Ms. Willis sighed. "As I was saying, I met your father then. He was a producer. He lived in San Francisco, and he was in town for a couple of weeks, trying to line up financing for some films. He asked me out, we had some great times together, and then he told me he was married."

"You had an *affair?* With a *married man?*" Suzanne felt as if she were losing her mind. She didn't know how much she could take in one day. It was bad enough that her mother had lied to her—now it turned out she was an illegitimate child, too? It was too sordid for words.

"I told you, I didn't know he was married until it was too late. We were already involved."

Ms. Willis paused, leaning forward. "Your father swore to me that his marriage was over, that he was going to get a divorce. He promised me things, Suzanne, and because I was young and naive, I believed him. He said we'd be together forever, that he'd make me a movie star, that we'd raise a family together . . . It was everything I'd ever wanted, or so I thought."

"So what went wrong?" Suzanne asked. She was unwillingly being drawn into her mother's story.

"He told me he would go back home and take care of everything. He asked me to give him enough time to break the news to his wife, then he'd be back. It might take a week, maybe a month, but he'd be back. He promised." Suzanne's mother stopped a moment. "I was prepared to wait for him, because I was in love," she went on. "About a week after he left, I found out I was pregnant."

"With me," Suzanne said.

Her mother nodded. "I was excited about having a baby with Steven. The timing was a little rough, but it seemed like it was meant to happen. The only problem was that when I tried to get in touch with Steven in San Francisco, where he said he lived, I couldn't find him. Not then, and not . . . ever."

"You never heard from him again?" Suzanne asked.

"No. And because of what he'd done to me, how he'd lied and deserted me when I needed him most, I didn't think it would help any if I told you about him. As far as I was concerned, he didn't exist. And that's why I told you he died in a car crash before you were born."

"So you're saying my father was a creep." Suzanne flinched at the thought. "I mean, it sure sounds that way to me. What kind of man would treat a woman like that? He had to be a total jerk."

"Well . . ." Ms. Willis hesitated. "He didn't handle the situation the way he should have. But maybe there's more to the story than that."

"Like what?" Suzanne demanded.

"Oh, I don't know. But maybe he had his reasons for not coming back to me. And you have to remember, he never knew I was pregnant. If he had, that might have changed everything," Suzanne's mother said. "Maybe he would have been more responsible."

Suzanne didn't say anything for a few moments. She tried to process the information her mother had just given her. She'd heard a lot, but it seemed as if there was twice as much she didn't know. "But Mom, if you never heard from him again, how do you know whether he's alive or dead? And if he was this big-time Hollywood producer, how come you couldn't find him? Why didn't you just show up at his studio or whatever?"

"Suzanne, believe me, I tried everything. Especially after you were born," Ms. Willis said. "But when somebody doesn't want to be found, he can manage it. Honey, you don't know how much I've wished he knew about you, how wonderful you are. He didn't leave me because of you—he didn't even know about you. You believe me, don't you?"

"Mom, I don't know what to believe," Suzanne said. "What about his family—his parents, my grandparents? Didn't you ever try to find him through them?"

"I didn't know where they were. I didn't know that much about him, only that I was head over heels in love for the first time in my life, and . . . I acted like a fool. I trusted him, and he walked away from me and never looked back. I've been struggling with that my whole life. Believe me, Suzanne, if I could have found him, I would have. It would have made our lives a lot easier."

"Why? Was he rich?" Suzanne asked. "Is that the only reason you wanted to find him—so I wouldn't be such a burden?"

"Yes, he's a very rich man," Valerie said. "But it had nothing to do with you being a burden, Suzanne, and you know it."

"You said he *is* a rich man. Then you know he's alive. Right?"

"I—I heard about him recently. Through an

old friend. Somebody who bumped into him."

"Is he still married?" Suzanne asked, sitting down next to her mother on the couch.

Valerie nodded. "Yes. And he has a family. That's all I know."

"What's his last name?"

"Carew. And that's the whole story, from beginning to end. I know I should have told you the truth, but since he walked out on me, it was easier for me to tell you that he'd died. I didn't want what he'd done to me to hurt you."

"Well, it's too late to stop me from getting hurt. I already *am* hurt. And it's all because of you!" Suzanne still couldn't believe it. Her father was alive somewhere, and he didn't even know that she existed. "Mom . . . are you sure there's nothing else you should tell me? Something else you've been meaning to tell me for sixteen years?" Suzanne realized how hurtful her tone of voice must sound, but she didn't care.

"No. That's everything," Ms. Willis said.

"Well, I hope so," Suzanne replied tersely. "Because it's more than enough to deal with, believe me." Her problems with Nikki, Victoria, and Luke seemed light-years away.

She had a father out there somewhere, and she was going to have to decide if she wanted to find him . . . the way her mother never had.

She wondered whether he was as much of a jerk as he seemed to be. Anyone who promised to come back and yet never showed his face again was probably not worth finding. Maybe she was better off without him, as her mother had thought.

But that's for me to decide now, Suzanne thought, watching her mother grab a water bottle from her desk and take a sip. Not Mom. It's time I took control of my own life for once.

"You know, I had no idea you were such a good kisser." John stepped back from Katia.

"Same here," Katia replied with a small smile. "Not until last night, anyway. But I always kind of suspected."

John grinned. "Really? Why's that?"

Katia could feel the blood rush to her face. "I don't know. I just always thought you'd be . . . great to kiss."

"You're blushing." John ran a finger gently down Katia's cheek. "Your cuteness factor is getting out of control here." He leaned closer and brushed her lips with a soft kiss, and then another.

Suddenly there was a loud bang as the door to the Steins' basement rec room flew open and the doorknob hit the wall. Katia and John jumped.

"Oh, ah, I'm sorry," Keith said, looking embarrassed by what he'd just seen. "I didn't mean to, uh, interrupt anything."

Katia turned around, John's arms still wrapped around her waist, her hands on his shoulders. Keith was staring at them with a dazed expression on his face, as if he'd seen a ghost.

He knows we just started dating, she thought. *Did he think we wouldn't kiss?* She knew Keith was having a hard time dealing with the fact that she was old enough to date now, and old enough to get involved with one of his best friends. Lately he'd been acting like such a big brother, it was ridiculous—as if she couldn't take care of herself!

"Sorry, guys. I didn't know you were down here," Keith went on.

"It's cool," John said, stepping away from Katia.

"Haven't you heard of knocking, Keith?" Katia asked, annoyed by the interruption.

"How was I supposed to know you guys were down here? Never mind what you'd be up to." Keith raised one eyebrow.

"It's okay. I was about to take off, anyway," John said.

"What about tonight? I thought we were going out," Katia said.

"I'll come back to pick you up later," John promised. "But my folks are expecting me home for dinner. It's our Sunday-night tradition."

Katia nodded. She knew that John's family was important to him. His mother was a veterinarian and his father was a lawyer, and they were very busy during the week, so they always made some weekend plans to spend time together. "Okay. Well, will you call me later, before you come to pick me up?"

"Definitely." John smiled at Katia, his dark brown eyes shining. He reached over and ruffled her long, wavy auburn hair with his hand. "See you, cutie."

"Bye," Katia said, smiling at him. He'd been calling her cutie since she was five, but now it was different. It felt familiar and yet romantic. They both knew she wasn't that same little girl anymore.

As soon as John ran up the stairs to leave, Keith turned to Katia. "Mind if I give you a little brotherly advice?"

"That depends," Katia said. "What is it?"

"Look, I know you've had a crush on John for a long time," Keith said, fiddling with the lamp on top of the bar.

"This isn't just a crush, Keith." Katia frowned. "It's a little more than that. We're dating each other—it's official now."

"Are you sure?" Keith asked.

"What do you mean by that?" Katia asked angrily.

"I know John, and I've seen the way he is with girls. He goes out with them for a week or two, then he dumps them. Hard," Keith said.

"That's not going to happen with me and John," Katia said. She couldn't believe Keith was assuming she was like those other girls. "John really cares about me."

"Right," Keith said sarcastically. "And how many seniors do you see dating sophomores?"

"Why are you saying all this, Keith?" Katia asked. She felt her eyes fill with tears, but she wouldn't give her brother the satisfaction of knowing he'd upset her. "John and I are getting along just fine, *without* your advice." How could she explain that John meant everything to her now, that before John started paying attention to her she'd felt as if she had nothing special, nothing to set her off as more than just Keith's little sister?

"I don't want to see you get your heart broken," Keith said. "John's hurt too many girls before."

"The only one who's hurting me is *you!*" Katia yelled as she ran out of the rec room.

Nothing like having an older brother around to ruin everything, she thought as she headed upstairs to her room.

Nothing was going to come between her and John—not another girl, not Keith, nothing, she thought as she went to her closet to pick out an outfit to wear to the movies that night. She would do anything to make sure of it.

Five

Suzanne woke up from her nap and glanced at the digital clock beside her bed. She felt weird and groggy. She almost never took naps, but when she'd gotten home from Willis Workout, she'd felt too emotionally drained to do anything but lie down on her bed. She must have fallen asleep. For a moment she thought she might have dreamed everything—Luke's kiss, Nikki's hatred, Victoria's accusations, her mother's lie . . .

I need to clear my head, Suzanne thought as she brushed out her brown hair and pulled it back into a ponytail.

She opened the window in her bedroom and breathed in the crisp air. The day was too beautiful to waste. She decided to go outside and get some exercise—that always made her feel better. It was too bad she didn't have anyone to go to Pequot State Park with, she thought at first, but then again, being alone sounded nice just then. Sometimes just walking in a peaceful place made everything seem better. I'll take my new mountain bike and ride as far as I can, she thought.

Suzanne knew better than to think that looking at the fall foliage would actually solve her problems, but at least it might take her mind off them for an hour or so.

"If one more mosquito comes near me, I'm turning around and going home. Aren't they supposed to be gone by now? I mean, it *is* the end of September already—shouldn't they be hibernating or something?"

Nikki laughed. "Victoria, mosquitoes don't hibernate."

"Yeah, that's right. They fly south for the winter," Deb Johnson added, laughing.

"Oh, very funny. I don't see any welts on either of you two." Victoria scratched at a bite on her hand.

Nikki took a deep breath of the woodsy air. She loved Pequot State Park in the early fall, when the leaves had just started to change and the air was crisp and clean.

Victoria shifted the small knapsack filled with drinks and snacks on her shoulder. "This thing weighs a ton. I think it's cutting off the circulation in my arm."

"Stop complaining already—it's not that bad," Deb said. "And stop thinking about everything that's wrong. Look around, it's a beautiful afternoon."

"The birds are singing, the sun is shining, blah, blah, blah," Victoria said. "Will you quit it already? I feel like we're in Girl Scouts. I really didn't want to go on a hike with Miss Positive, Motivated, and Well-Adjusted."

"Oh, and I'm just loving this hike with Queen Victoria," Deb retorted. "Next thing you know, you'll be asking us to carry you the rest of the way so you don't get blisters on your feet."

"Just cool it, you guys, okay? We came up here to have fun, not argue," Nikki said, shaking her head. She knew they were kidding around, not really fighting.

Deb and Victoria were her best friends in Hillcrest, but they couldn't be more different. Victoria preferred the hottest fashions and was so caught up in her appearance, she seemed conceited. Deb was just as pretty, with dark brown skin and shoulder-length hair, but she didn't play up her looks. She was petite, and tended to wear preppie-type clothes. Deb looked as though she'd just walked off an Ivy League campus, whereas Victoria often dressed as though she was about to go out to a

New York City club and dance the night away.

And as far as boys and dating were concerned, Victoria and Deb were opposites as well. Victoria was bold around guys and almost never spent a weekend without a date. But Deb had never gone out with any guy, had never even kissed anyone at school or during the summers she spent with her parents and brother at their beach house. Sometimes Nikki was amazed that Victoria and Deb could get along at all.

"Do you guys want to stop and eat?" Deb asked. "I'm starving."

"I'd love an apple," Nikki said. "We brought some, didn't we?"

"I'll check." Victoria swung the knapsack off her shoulder and reached inside.

Nikki could hear the Pequot River rushing by, just to the west of them. She'd have to go look at the river after they ate; she loved the sound of the water splashing over the rocks on its way toward the waterfall that dropped down the incline they'd just climbed up.

Actually, Nikki had a private spot, not too far from where they were standing, to which she often went when she was trying to sort things out in her life. She'd found it one day when she was about eight years old, and had been using it ever since as her own special hideaway. Sometimes she sat and read. Other times she listened to the sounds of the woods as she thought about stuff. Sometimes she turned up her Walkman, blasting the music through her headphones, and tuned out the world.

Maybe I should have come up here by myself today, she thought briefly. She took a bandanna out of her jeans pocket and wiped the sweat off her forehead.

She was about to sit down next to Victoria and Deb when she heard the sound of a bicycle shifting gears. A few seconds later Suzanne appeared from around a curve in the path, riding her mountain bike toward them.

Oh, no. Nikki cringed. She didn't want to see Suzanne again. She'd been having such a good time, she'd almost forgotten how upset she'd been feeling.

"Well, if it isn't the boyfriend stealer from Brooklyn," Victoria said as Suzanne reached the top of the hill.

"Hi," Suzanne said, panting from the exertion of riding up such a steep incline. She glanced hopefully at Nikki, but Nikki looked away.

Victoria took a long drink out of a bottle of spring water. "Gee, I don't think we packed enough drinks for four," she said sarcastically. "Sorry. But if you're thirsty, the river's right over there."

"Victoria! What's wrong with you?" Deb said, sounding shocked by her friend's rudeness. "Hi, Suzanne. Wow, you rode all the way up that hill? You must be in great shape." She offered Suzanne her bottle of water, but Suzanne shook her head.

"I spend a lot of time working out at my mom's gym," Suzanne said as she removed her own bottle from its holder on the bike. She took a swallow, then put the bottle back into its holder. "Hi, Nikki," Suzanne said tentatively. "How's it going?"

"About the same," Nikki said curtly.

Suzanne nodded. "I was going to call you later to—"

"Don't bother," Nikki interrupted.

"Please, Nikki, I—"

"Can't you take a hint? Do I have to spell it out for you? I don't want to talk to you!" Nikki yelled. But Suzanne didn't move. Nikki took a step backward. If Suzanne wasn't going to get the message and take off, then she would. She turned and started making her way through the woods, pushing hemlock branches out of her way.

"Nikki, wait!" Suzanne called after her.

"Leave her alone!" Victoria shouted at Suzanne. "Can't you see she's had enough of you and your phony I'm-your-best-friend act?"

"It's *not* phony," Suzanne said. "Not that I'd expect you to know anything about real friendship!"

"Whoa, guys," Deb said. "You don't have to

yell at each other. I don't really know what's going on here, but I'm sure we can find a way to work this out."

"Yeah, I have a great idea," Victoria said. "How about if *she* moves back to Brooklyn?"

Nikki could hear them arguing as she ran away. Then she heard the sounds of the three girls crashing through the brush behind her and thought, Great, now I've got the entire cavalry coming after me!

But Nikki had no intention of letting them find her. She headed for her secret hideaway, then changed her mind. She'd walk along the river instead.

She hoped the other girls weren't still following as she ran toward the water's edge. She wished they'd all just go home and leave her alone. Her whole afternoon was ruined now, anyway.

As she got closer the sound of rushing water filled her ears. She watched the changing colors of the river as it cascaded over rocks, around bends, and down to the waterfall below. She'd loved coming to the river ever since she was a kid—it was exciting and soothing at the same time.

I'll go farther downstream. They'll never find me there, she thought. She dodged around a bush and moved closer to the water's edge. There was no path there, so Nikki hopped from rock to rock. She saw a red leaf swirling in the current. It was caught in a powerful whirlpool, and she watched as it was sucked under the water's surface.

"Nikki!"

At the faint cry from behind her, she glanced over her shoulder as she continued to run. She didn't see the wet rock just in front of her—and then she screamed as her foot slipped and, before she could catch herself, she tumbled right into the river!

It's freezing! Nikki thought. Her fingertips felt numb already. She scrambled, trying to touch bottom with her feet. But it was too deep, and the current was already dragging her toward the middle of the river. She tried to swim toward shore . . . and that was when she realized how fast she was traveling. In just a few seconds she had been swept several yards downstream.

She saw a tree trunk leaning out over the water and stretched her arms practically out of their sockets trying to reach it. Her fingers brushed against the rough bark, but the current whipped her past the tree before she could grab on to it. Her chin dipped below the surface of the water, and she swallowed a mouthful of water. With an effort she lifted her head farther out of the water, sputtering and choking.

I'm going to drown! she thought, panicking.

I'm going to die! She flailed her arms in the water, desperately trying to grab hold of something. "Help me! Somebody help me!" she screamed as loudly as she could. Then suddenly a branch floating downstream hit her in the face and knocked her head underwater.

Six

"What was that?" Deb asked.

"It sounded like somebody screaming," Suzanne said, hoping she was mistaken but at the same time knowing she wasn't.

"It's Nikki," Victoria said breathlessly.

Suzanne ran faster, the other two girls right behind her. "It's coming from over here!" They rushed to the water's edge, but Nikki was nowhere in sight.

"Help!"

They all stopped and stood where they were, looking around as they heard another faint cry.

"She's definitely in the water somewhere," Deb said. "But where? I can't see her."

Suzanne jogged down to the rocky bank and around the bend in the river. If Nikki had fallen into the water, Suzanne reasoned, she would have been pulled downstream. She scanned the water's surface. Nothing. All Suzanne could see were rocks and floating leaves.

Then, just as she was about to give up, she spotted Nikki's long blond hair streaming in the water. "Nikki!" she screamed. "Over here!" she yelled to the other girls.

Deb and Victoria came running. "Where?"

"There!" Suzanne pointed to a rock on the far side of the river. Nikki was clinging to it for dear life. "Nikki," she called to her, "try to pull yourself up!"

"I can't!" Nikki wailed. A trickle of blood was running down her face. "Every time I try to move, I feel like I'm going to lose my grip. And if I lose my grip—" She glanced over her shoulder at the waterfall just twenty feet downstream.

"She's in trouble," Deb said. "Big trouble. What can we do?"

"Why can't she just swim to shore?" Victoria asked, as if that were the most obvious solution in the world.

"The current's too strong," Suzanne answered. "She can barely hold on where she is, never mind swim against it."

"I'll go for help!" Deb yelled, already taking off through the woods, back to the path.

"Take my bike!" Suzanne called after her.

"And hurry!" Victoria yelled. Then she turned back to the river. "Nikki, hold on! We're going to get you out!"

"Are you okay?" Suzanne yelled again.

"I'm freezing!" Nikki replied, her wet blond hair sticking to her face. "I can't hold on much longer."

"Don't let go, Nikki! Whatever you do, don't let go!" Victoria screamed hysterically.

"Don't scare her," Suzanne whispered to Victoria. "She's panicking enough as it is. Keep talking to her, but calmly. Make sure she doesn't give up and let go."

Victoria nodded. "Nikki, hold on! As soon as we get you out of that river, we'll go on a major shopping spree!" She jumped up and down and waved to Nikki.

Then she turned to Suzanne, a single tear running down her face. "What if she can't hold on?" she asked.

Suzanne watched Nikki's body bob in the water with each surge of the current. She didn't answer.

"Where's Deb? It seems like she's been gone forever," Victoria went on, sounding sick with impatience.

Suzanne suddenly pulled off her shoes and ran into the river. She couldn't just stand on the bank and watch Nikki lose her already weakened grip. It was her fault that Nikki had run off and slipped into the river. If Nikki died, it would be all because of her.

The bank dropped off sharply, and in a moment the frigid water was over Suzanne's waist.

"Suzanne! Wait! What if—" Victoria didn't finish the sentence, but Suzanne knew what she was going to say: What if you both drown?

Suzanne dove in and swam as hard as she could toward Nikki. She'd started upstream from her, so the drag of the current helped pull her toward Nikki at first. Then she had to fight it with all her might just to move a few feet to her right, across the current. I bet Mom never thought my swimming lessons would prepare me for this, she thought, straining as hard as she could to gain a few inches. It was like trying to swim through the middle of a powerful whirlpool.

Then, suddenly, she was in a pocket of still water with no current to drag her. Suzanne paddled as fast as she could, and she reached Nikki a few seconds later. She was exhausted from the short, intense swim, but she knew she was much better off than Nikki.

"Nikki, you're bleeding! What happened?" she asked, stopping beside her friend and immediately grabbing the same rock Nikki was clinging to. The current was stronger in this section of the river and threatened to pull them both downstream.

"A branch," Nikki gasped. "It—it—"

"Never mind, you can tell me later," Suzanne told her, steadying herself against the rock with one hand as she reached out for Nikki with her other hand. "Here—I'm going to wrap my arm around your shoulders, and we're going to swim to the near side, right there. It's only fifteen feet or so—we can make it."

"Suzanne, I'm too cold . . . too tired," Nikki said. "I can't make it."

"I'll swim for both of us," Suzanne said. "I'll pull you. We're going to be okay."

Suzanne crooked her arm around Nikki's shoulder and across her chest. Then she pushed off the rock with both feet. She stroked determinedly through the water with one arm, pulling Nikki with the other. She had never worked so hard at anything in her life.

The icy cold sent sharp pains through her quickly numbing body, and Suzanne lost her momentum for a second. Nikki's head went underwater as Suzanne struggled to right herself and keep swimming. For a brief second she thought they weren't going to make it. Instead of saving Nikki, she was going to end up killing them both. Then Suzanne heard Nikki cough as her mouth and nostrils emerged from the water and she spat out the water that had rushed into her mouth. Suzanne knew she couldn't let Nikki die. She couldn't give up.

Somehow she found the strength to make it the last couple of yards. Then her feet touched the rocky bottom of the river and she stood up, fighting the current with her legs as she dragged Nikki to shore.

Victoria ran toward them. "Thank goodness you're both okay! I've never been so worried in my entire life! It was like a scene out of a rescue show, only I think I'd rather see dramatic reenactments from now on. The real thing is too horrible to watch!"

Suzanne gripped Nikki around her waist and helped her stand. Together they climbed up across the rocks and collapsed on a small patch of grass. Suzanne lay there on the ground, exhausted. Nikki was coughing up water.

"Nikki, say something," Victoria urged.

"I'm okay," she managed just as Deb and a uniformed park ranger appeared on the other side of the river.

Victoria stood up and waved her arms. "Over here!" she yelled. "We're over here! Hurry!"

Nikki could barely feel her hands when the park ranger put a wool blanket over her and told her to keep her arms wrapped around herself. Then, when she could feel them, her palms throbbed with pain from where she'd been gripping the rock. She glanced down at her fingers and saw that the skin had been rubbed off in some places.

"I'm so glad you're both okay," Deb said. "When I took off down the hill on your bike, Suzanne, I was afraid I wouldn't be fast enough."

"At least you didn't have to watch it," Victoria said. "I nearly had a heart attack. There was this one second when Suzanne stopped swimming and I thought they were both going under for good." She launched into a description of the rescue for Deb, which Nikki only partly heard. Her head felt so foggy, she couldn't pay attention. She could only vaguely remember running away from Suzanne, slipping on the wet rock, and plunging into the strong, cold current.

"Suzanne," Nikki panted, her teeth chattering as the park ranger wrapped another blanket around her shoulders, "you saved my life. I never would have made it without you. How . . . why . . . why did you—"

"Shh, it's okay now," Suzanne said, grasping the blanket around her own shoulders with one hand as she rubbed Nikki's arm. "Just concentrate on warming up."

"She's right," the park ranger said. "You need to get your blood circulating again. The paramedics will be here soon."

"Suzanne . . ." Nikki's voice trailed off. How could she begin to thank Suzanne for what she'd done? Suzanne had risked her life to save her after Nikki had refused even to listen to her that morning. "I have to thank you. I have to—"

"You don't have to do anything," Suzanne said, shivering. "I'm just glad you're safe. Nothing else matters, okay?"

"No, it does. I shouldn't have—"

"Here they are!" The park ranger stood up and called to the paramedics. The next thing Nikki knew, she was being whisked onto a stretcher and a paramedic was leaning over her, examining the cut on her face.

She felt more blankets being wrapped around her, and slowly she stopped shaking. Then, before she could say or do anything else, her mind went blank, and she was enveloped in darkness.

Thank God Nikki's okay, Victoria thought as she sped around a curve in the road on her way home. I don't know what I'd do without her.

Victoria still could hardly believe what had almost happened that afternoon. All they'd wanted to do was spend an afternoon outdoors. Next thing she knew, her best friend was on the verge of drowning. Victoria was grateful to Suzanne—not that she'd ever admit it. Maybe Suzanne was a fraud, but at least she was a good swimmer.

She turned off the engine, got out of the car, and ran up the walk to her house. Her parents' cars were always in the two-car garage, and she'd stopped complaining about never getting a spot. As her father had told her a hundred times, she was lucky they'd even given her a car—he sure wasn't going to hand over his precious garage door opener.

Victoria reached the front door, but before she could put her key in the lock, the door swung open. Her father stood on the threshold, wearing one of his double-breasted Italian suits, his graying brown hair slicked back with gel. He was frowning, a glass in his hand as usual. "Where have you been?" he demanded.

"Daddy, you're not going to believe what happened," Victoria said, walking past him into the foyer.

"What I don't believe is how late you are," Mr. Hill said. "We were supposed to be at Mayor Norris's house over an hour ago. Or don't you remember?"

"Daddy! Just wait and hear what I have to say," Victoria argued, putting her purse on the glass coffee table in the living room. "I didn't forget—I came home as soon as I could. We were hiking over at Pequot, and then Nikki fell into the river and—"

"You don't need to tell me any more." Mr. Hill shook his head. "I've heard enough. All I need to know is that while I was waiting for you to find the time to show up, you were hiking with your friends. Victoria, I've told you again and again how important it is for me to make a good showing at anything even remotely connected to politics in this town. I need the mayor on my side if I'm ever going to get those zoning laws changed. I can't believe you'd pull something like this!" Mr. Hill took a gulp of his drink.

"Daddy, it was an emergency," Victoria said, nervously watching him refill his glass at the bar in the corner of the living room. How could he fault her for going to the hospital to make sure her friend was all right? "You know I'd never—"

"I'll tell you what an emergency is," her father interrupted angrily. "An emergency is not showing up when the mayor invites you and your family to dinner. *That's* an emergency. Your mother is there now, making excuses for us, and I—"

"So why did you wait for me? Why didn't you just make an excuse?" Victoria asked. You should be used to making excuses by now, she felt like saying. How many times had she heard him beg out of social occasions or call in sick to work, all because he was too drunk or too hung over from the night before?

"Because I thought you might show up only

a few minutes late, and we'd simply meet your mother and your sister there," Mr. Hill said.

Victoria had heard enough. "Daddy, Nikki almost *died.* Did you expect me to run out on her?"

"You were the one who saved her?" he asked.

"Well, I didn't jump into the water myself, but—"

"So you didn't do much besides just stand there!" Mr. Hill sneered. "I doubt whether Nikki knew you were there at all, that's how much it sounds like you helped."

How does he always know which buttons to push to hurt me the most? Victoria wondered. As if she didn't feel guilty enough about not saving her best friend. "Daddy, if I'd jumped in, it only would have made things worse. I could see that Suzanne was doing fine, and—"

"And so you did nothing? Congratulations, Victoria! Nice going!" He shifted his glass and clapped his hands lightly together in mock applause. "What do you think that does to my reputation, Victoria? Your best friend is near death, and you're simply watching from the sidelines! At least if you were going to miss the dinner, you could have impressed the mayor with your heroism—but no, someone else's daughter jumped in to save Nikki's life while you just stood there. What were you doing, Victoria, filing your nails?"

"Shut up, Daddy!" Victoria screamed. She couldn't take his badgering any longer. She felt bad enough about not being the one who'd rescued Nikki; why did he have to rub it in? Besides, was it her fault she wasn't a strong swimmer? "You don't know anything about it! Stop criticizing me for—"

Victoria fell silent as her father moved toward her. He set his glass down on the coffee table. "Don't ever tell me to shut up, young lady."

"I didn't mean to yell. I'm just upset, Daddy. Nikki—"

"And stop using Nikki Stewart as an excuse for your pathetic mistake this afternoon," Mr. Hill seethed. "You've ruined everything I've worked so hard for. Are you proud of yourself?"

"I haven't ruined anything," Victoria said. She wasn't going to be blamed for her father's downward-spiraling career. "If anyone's ruined things for you, it's yourself! Why don't you try to make it through one day without drinking yourself into oblivion?"

"Go upstairs and get ready to meet the mayor," he said fiercely. "You've got five minutes to look your best."

Victoria dashed up the stairs, went into her

room, and slammed the door as loudly as she could. She knew it was childish, but she couldn't help herself. How many times had her father gotten drunk and then turned against her? She was losing track.

She stared at her face in the mirror above her dresser. Her cheeks were tearstained. She didn't know how much more of her father's drunken routine she could take. But one thing she knew for sure—she wouldn't ever let him see her cry again.

Seven

"Where's Nikki Stewart? I have to see her right away!" Luke Martinson stood at the information desk on the first floor of Hillcrest Community Hospital. He drummed his fingers against the counter as the woman behind the desk slowly put down the supermarket tabloid she was intently reading.

"How do you spell that?" the clerk asked, popping the chewing gum in her mouth.

"Stewart?" Luke asked, incredulous. "You know, *Stewart*. S-t-e-w-"

"Her *first* name, please," the woman said in an irritated voice.

"N-i-k-k-i," Luke said. "She almost drowned at Pequot Park."

"Are you a family member?" the woman asked, sounding bored as she punched the information into the computer and stared at the screen. "Because our visiting hours are—"

"Oh, forget it." Luke turned and jogged down the hall toward the sign that said Emergency, his black motorcycle boots clomping loudly against the vinyl floor. He wasn't about to let an incompetent keep him from seeing Nikki—he wasn't about to let anything stop him.

"Wait, you can't do that!" the woman behind the information desk protested.

"Watch me!" Luke called over his shoulder as he turned the corner at the end of the hall. He had to find Nikki. If she died before he had a chance to tell her how much he loved her, he wouldn't be able to live with himself. He hoped he wasn't already too late.

He raced down another corridor and almost collided with an empty wheelchair. Then he saw her. Nikki was lying motionless on a gurney. An orderly was wheeling her into a small examination room. *She's alive!* he realized as he got a better look. But she didn't look okay. Her eyes were closed, and the left side of her face was red and puffy. "Nikki?" he said softly, keeping pace with the moving gurney.

"Look, I'm not sure who you are, but you can't disturb the patients," the orderly began.

"Nikki, are you all right? Say something," Luke pleaded desperately, ignoring the hostile glare from the orderly.

"Luke?" Nikki opened her eyes and looked up at him. "Is that you, Luke?"

"You're okay!" Luke exclaimed, impulsively leaning over to kiss her cheek before he remembered that she was angry at him and might not appreciate it. He stood up straight again and looked at her nervously. "I was so worried—I had to come down and see if you were all right."

"How did you know . . . ?" Nikki began, looking confused.

"I was at work, and Deb called to tell me. She said you'd been unconscious." Luke shuddered now, remembering how scared he'd felt when he heard the news.

"Only for a few seconds," Nikki said. "I guess I fainted when I realized what almost happened to me. The waterfall . . . I almost . . ."

"Don't think about it now," Luke said as the orderly wheeled Nikki into a room and stopped. "So is she okay now?" he asked the man.

"She checked out fine, as far as I know," the orderly replied. "The doctor wants to put something on her face laceration, and then she'll probably be released."

"Then I'll wait for the doctor with her," Luke said. "It's okay, you can take off."

"Sorry, no can do," the orderly said. "You shouldn't even be down here in the first place. You'll have to wait outside just like everyone else." He took Luke by the shoulders and guided him toward the door.

"Nikki, I'll be right outside!" Luke cried as the orderly opened the door and pushed him out into the hall. "Easy, buddy. You don't need to impress me with your muscles," he muttered, shaking the man's hands off his arm.

He turned and practically bumped right into Suzanne, who was walking down the hall with a nurse. At first he didn't recognize her, since she was wearing the same kind of hospital gown Nikki had on. But even that shapeless garment looked great on Suzanne's tall, leggy form.

Luke felt completely flustered. He didn't know what to say to Suzanne—or whether he should say anything at all. He hadn't seen or spoken to her since their poorly timed kiss on the golf course the night before, and the sight of her made his heart beat faster. He tried to squelch the feelings he had for Suzanne. He hadn't lied when he told her how he felt about her. But now he realized he couldn't leave Nikki. Especially after she'd almost died.

Still, he wanted to say something to Suzanne. He couldn't talk about the night before, but he had to at least thank her for saving Nikki's life. To tell her she must have been brave to jump into the Pequot to save another person.

But by the time Luke had mustered his

courage to speak, Suzanne had already passed him and was halfway to the waiting room. As he watched her walk away she turned and glanced in his direction. She smiled briefly at him, then continued on her way without saying a word.

So that's how it's going to be, Luke thought, slowly following Suzanne. She apparently wanted to put their brief little fling behind her as much as he did. He didn't know whether to feel relief or disappointment. He'd felt such a connection with Suzanne. She seemed to be the only person who really understood him. They had a lot in common, and she was beautiful, too, similar to Nikki, only darker, more mysterious.

Not everything in Suzanne's life had come easily for her. She didn't have rich, powerful parents to buy her whatever she wanted—not like Nikki and her friends, who'd never had to worry about a thing. He wondered if Suzanne felt a connection between them, too.

But he told himself that all he should be thinking about at the moment was Nikki and how he'd almost lost her. She was the one good thing he had going for him right now. He didn't know what he would do with his life without Nikki in it. He'd have nothing—less than nothing.

That was why he'd decided he was never

going to take a chance on losing Nikki again . . . even if it meant fighting his attraction to Suzanne.

Suzanne sat down on a blue plastic chair in the waiting room. "Your mother should be here any second," the nurse said, handing Suzanne a bag with her sopping-wet clothes. "She'll have some dry clothes for you. You're sure you feel okay? Are you warm enough? I can get you a blanket."

"Thanks. I'm fine," Suzanne said. Through the doorway she saw Luke outside, pacing back and forth almost as if he were afraid to come in and sit down in the same room with her. He didn't have to worry—she wasn't going to make a move on him. She wouldn't even talk to him unless Nikki was around. She couldn't believe he was already at the hospital—she and Nikki had been brought in only about a half hour earlier, and not even her mother had made it yet.

"I'm fine. I feel a hundred percent normal." She paused. "Do you think it'd be okay if I went in and talked to Nikki? I know she's not supposed to have any visitors except for family, but—"

"I'm sure she considers you family after what you did for her today," the nurse said with a smile. "Go ahead."

Considers me family? I doubt it. But maybe we can start over again, Suzanne thought as she slowly pushed open the door. She took a deep breath. "Nikki? Can I come in?" she asked, knocking lightly on the half-open door.

"Suzanne?" Nikki asked, propping herself up on her elbows. "Sure. Come on in."

"Hi." Suzanne walked over to the bed. "Are they done with you yet?"

"Yeah, except for all the paperwork, I guess." Nikki touched the gauze bandage on her cheek. "This is attractive, isn't it? Too bad Halloween's a month away. I could wrap the rest of myself up like this and make a perfect mummy."

Suzanne laughed. "You don't look that bad."

"So, you're okay, right?" Nikki asked. "I mean, you look fine."

"You know, they say swimming in incredibly cold water does wonders for the complexion," Suzanne joked.

Nikki smiled. "Cool outfit, by the way. We look like twins. Maybe we should audition for roles as patients on that new hospital soap opera . . . I forget the name of it, though."

"Hey, that would be fun." Suzanne smiled back. "My clothes are still soaked. Maybe they'll let us wear these gowns home. We can start a new fashion trend."

There was a moment of awkward silence.

Suzanne wasn't sure if she should stay or leave. She moved toward the door until Nikki said, "Wait, Suzanne, there's something I want to—"

"Nikki!" The door flew open, and Nikki's father rushed into the room. "Are you okay, honey? What were you doing in that river? Haven't I told you a million times not to swim in—"

"Dad, I didn't jump in, I fell in," Nikki told him, laughing as he hugged her tightly. "And I never would have gotten out alive if it hadn't been for Suzanne."

Mr. Stewart turned from the hospital bed and focused on Suzanne. "Yes, that's what I just heard on the local radio station. They're calling you the hero of Hillcrest."

"How embarrassing," Suzanne said. "Couldn't they come up with something more original? They make me sound like a comic-book superhero."

"Superhero or not, you saved my daughter's life," Mr. Stewart continued. "And I'm extremely grateful." He walked over to Suzanne and held out his hand. Then, just as she was about to shake his hand, he pulled her close to him and hugged her awkwardly. "You have no idea how much this means to me."

Suzanne stepped back from Mr. Stewart as he released her. She'd never been hugged so hard in her entire life.

"Thanks again," he said, still holding on to her hand.

"You're welcome," she said. She felt uncomfortable, but she could understand how emotional Nikki's father must be feeling. "It was no big—"

"Suzanne! You're all right!" Ms. Willis rushed into the room with Ian's father right behind her. Suzanne knew they'd had a date after her mother's aerobics class, but she was surprised that Mr. Houghton had come with her mom to the hospital.

Suzanne was about to reassure her mother that she was all right when Ms. Willis turned and noticed Mr. Stewart standing beside Nikki's hospital bed. Suzanne watched as her mother's expression changed from relief to something else—anger?

"Mom, this is Nikki's father," Suzanne said, hoping no one else noticed how rudely her mother was staring at him. "Mr. Stewart, my mother, Valerie Willis."

"Yes," Mr. Stewart said coldly. "We've met."

"Mr. Stewart is a . . . a member at the studio," Suzanne's mother said, regaining her composure a little. "A regular member, actually. How's the weight training going?"

"Oh—" Mr. Stewart coughed. "Just fine. Don't worry about me. Actually, all we should be thinking about right now are our girls."

"How are you feeling?" Suzanne's mother went over to Nikki. "Are you all right?"

Nikki nodded. "Thanks to Suzanne, I'm fine."

"And you?" Ms. Willis slowly approached Suzanne. Since their argument that morning, Ms. Willis was afraid of how Suzanne would react to her. "I was so worried when they paged me at the restaurant. I couldn't stand it if you were hurt for even one second."

"I'm fine, Mom," Suzanne said. "No scratches, no lingering hypothermia." She was embarrassed by all the attention she was getting. She wished she could be alone with Nikki and make sure that Nikki had forgiven her, that everything could go back to the way it had been before.

"Was the water really that cold?" Mr. Stewart asked. "I wouldn't think it would be that bad this time of year."

"Dad, why don't *you* jump in next weekend and tell me what you think?" Nikki said, and Suzanne laughed. "My hands were frozen solid when Suzanne pulled me out."

"Did you take a lifesaving course?" Ian's father asked Suzanne.

"Excuse me . . . Mr. Willis? Mrs. Stewart?" A nurse poked her head through the door.

Mr. Stewart cleared his throat. "It's the other way around, actually. I'm Mr. Stewart, and this is Ms. Willis."

"Oh—sorry." The nurse blushed. "Could you both come with me? We need to get the insurance forms filled out, and then the girls can go."

"I'll go, too," Mr. Houghton said. "I'm glad you girls are okay."

"Thanks," Suzanne said, smiling at him.

There was an awkward silence after the adults had left the hospital room.

Finally Nikki spoke. "You know, if anyone had told me this morning that you'd be the one to end up saving my life, I wouldn't have believed them." Her voice was thick with emotion. "I really thought you were out to get me. Maybe I listened to Victoria too much."

"No, you had every right not to trust me, after the stupid thing I did," Suzanne said. It hit Suzanne that neither one of them had mentioned Luke's name.

"Well, yeah, you're right—I did. But the point is, I know now that I can trust you. You risked your life today to save me. You didn't have to do that. You could have waited for the park ranger to show up, or—"

"Nikki! I couldn't have stood there and waited, knowing how close you were to losing your grip. Look, I know I haven't acted like a good friend to you recently, but I promise that if you give me another chance, I won't let you down again."

"I know," Nikki said, close to tears. "I know you won't. Today proved that."

"So . . . can we go back to being friends, and try to forget about the bad stuff?" Suzanne asked nervously. She felt as if she was about to start crying, too.

Nikki nodded. "Definitely. And if you ever need me, I'm here for you."

Suzanne leaned over and gave Nikki a big hug. "Thanks. It helps, knowing I can count on you. I feel alone a lot of the time, you know?"

"It must be hard," Nikki said. "Especially after what Victoria told you this morning."

"Oh, yeah, *that* small detail. My mother tried to explain it to me, but I don't know. It doesn't add up. I don't think she's told me the whole truth yet," Suzanne admitted.

"Really? Why?" Nikki prompted.

"Well, she said she—" Suzanne stopped as the door opened and Luke stepped into the room.

"Sorry—I didn't mean to interrupt," he said. "It's just that there's a reporter out here who wants to talk to Suzanne, and she's getting pretty impatient."

"She wants to talk to me?" Suzanne repeated. "I guess today's a slow news day. I'll see you later, Nikki, okay?" Suzanne wasn't especially eager to talk to the reporter, but she was even less happy about staying in the same room with Luke and Nikki. She headed for the door, while Luke moved closer to Nikki. They brushed past each other awkwardly. Suzanne felt her skin tingle where Luke's arm had accidentally touched hers. She longed to keep contact between her and Luke, but she knew that was impossible. That's the way it's going to be from now on, she told herself. Nikki and Luke belong together. And I'm not going to interfere anymore.

"Hey, Suzanne?" Luke said as she opened the door to leave.

She turned to face both of them and managed the brightest, most nonchalant smile she could despite the sight of Luke's arm around Nikki's shoulder. "Yeah?"

"Thanks a lot. For saving Nikki, I mean," Luke quickly added.

"Sure." Suzanne waved at Nikki. "Take care."

Luke had already turned back to his girlfriend and was kissing her tenderly. Suzanne looked away, but it was too late—she'd already seen them. It was as if a stake had been thrust through Suzanne's heart. But Luke and Nikki were so enthralled with each other that they didn't notice the expression on her face.

As tears sprang to her eyes Suzanne crept

silently from the room. She stood in the hallway as the door drifted closed behind her, until she heard the latch click. She knew she was doing the right thing, walking away from any chance she had with Luke.

Luke Martinson wasn't a part of her future; he was a part of her past. He belonged with Nikki.

Eight

Victoria stared at the headline in Monday morning's *Hillcrest Herald*. "Newcomer Makes Daring Rescue: Saves High-School Friend from Certain Disaster."

"Certain disaster," Victoria muttered to herself, frowning at a photo of Suzanne. "Nikki would have been fine if Suzanne hadn't chased her. Nikki fell into the river just because she was trying to get away from her!"

She skimmed the article, searching for a reference to herself. Nothing. The reporter had stuffed the story full of gushing compliments about Suzanne from Nikki, Nikki's family, and apparently anyone else she'd bothered to stop on the street on the way back to her office. It was almost enough to make Victoria lose her appetite.

But she picked the last piece of croissant off her plate and put it in her mouth, careful not to smudge her lipstick. She wasn't going to let Suzanne's so-called heroism get her down. Nikki would see soon enough what Suzanne was really made of.

Normally Victoria hated Mondays, but she was glad this particular weekend was over. In fact, the less said about her weekend, the better. It had been a total disaster on all fronts. She was actually relieved that she'd have to leave for school in ten minutes.

"Princess?"

Victoria stood up and hurried to put her plate in the sink. There was no way her father could be drunk this early in the morning, but she still didn't want to talk to him. Not after everything that had happened the day before. "Daddy, I'm on my way out the door. If I don't leave in two seconds, I'll be late for school," she lied hastily when he came into the kitchen.

"This will only take a minute," Mr. Hill said, setting a small white box on the counter. "First, I want to say how sorry I am about what happened yesterday. I realize I got so caught up in worrying about my own life that I was very hard on you."

"Let's not talk about it, okay?" Victoria turned the newspaper she'd been reading facedown on the kitchen table. "I've already forgotten." Just like I've forgotten all the other times you've been rotten to me and then apologized. It's becoming a regular routine.

"Well, I haven't," Mr. Hill continued. "And I certainly haven't forgotten how charming you were yesterday at the mayor's dinner. We may have been late, but you certainly made an entrance. I just want to say . . . thank you." He slid the box toward Victoria. "Here. This is for you. I was going to give this to you on your birthday, but I want you to have it now. I'll just have to get you something else on your birthday."

"Daddy, you don't—"

"Just open it," Mr. Hill said.

Victoria shrugged and lifted the cover of the box. Inside, lying on a black velveteen pad, was a diamond tennis bracelet, sparkling in the light from the overhead lamp. Victoria gasped and lifted it out of the box. "It's beautiful," she said.

"Not nearly as beautiful as you, but it was the best I could do." Her father leaned closer and kissed her on the cheek. "Have a great day at school—I'll see you tonight."

He left the kitchen, and Victoria stood there in a daze, listening to him start his Jaguar in the garage.

She fondled the bracelet, which was a peace offering, just like all the other jewelry she had upstairs in the case on her dresser.

Each time it was something nicer, something more extravagant.

Well, at least Daddy has good taste, she thought as she fastened the bracelet around her wrist.

As always, it seemed as if no one was eager to enter the school building on Monday morning. A lot of kids were hanging out near the front steps, waiting for the bell to ring before going inside.

Ian was helping his cousin Sally Ross with her math homework.

"Nothing like waiting till the last minute, Sal," Ian said. "Quadratic equations aren't really that tough once you get the basics down."

"What can I say? I missed basic training," Sally quipped.

"Not bad." Ian smiled. "But not good, either."

"Well, they can't all be gems." Sally finished jotting down the answer to the last problem. "Thanks for the help."

"No prob." Ian stuffed his math textbook into his backpack and stood up just as Victoria sauntered over.

As usual, Victoria was dressed to kill, in a short black miniskirt, a fuzzy mauve angora sweater, thigh-high stockings, and a pair of shiny black walking boots.

"Look what the cat dragged in," Sally

whispered, loudly enough for Victoria to hear.

Victoria wasn't thrilled to see Sally, either. She was hoping to have a few minutes alone with Ian, even though their date Saturday night had been a disaster. She thought if she got him away from his computer, things might heat up between them. Maybe a movie . . .

But she couldn't very well make her move on Ian with Sally sitting right there. Sally always had something obnoxious to say to Victoria—and always pretended it was a joke. But the only thing funny about Sally Ross as far as Victoria was concerned was her clothes. Victoria had seen better-dressed bag ladies.

Victoria hadn't been able to stand Sally even before she decided she wanted to go out with Ian. But now Sally was even more in the way. *Maybe if I ignore her,* Victoria figured, *she'll take the hint and leave.* "Hi, Ian," she said as she dropped her leather knapsack near his feet. "You're not leaving, are you? I just got here."

"Uh, actually, I have to get to homeroom early." Ian picked up his backpack and headed toward the entrance to the school.

"Okay, well, see you later," Victoria called after him, disappointed. He'd barely looked at her—and she had spent almost an hour that morning putting together her outfit. Maybe she was going about this all wrong, she decided. She didn't really know Ian that well . . . but Sally did. Maybe Sally could help her figure out a way to snag Ian.

Sally had finished putting her homework away and now started adjusting a buckle on her Birkenstocks. Victoria seized her chance. "Uh, Sally, do you know where I can get a pair of sandals like yours?" she asked.

"I thought I was the comedian around here." Sally paused. "Are you serious?"

"I just thought maybe I'd try something different. Change my look a little."

"You mean to catch a look from Ian, right?" Sally said, wiggling her eyebrows suggestively.

"Maybe," Victoria responded noncommittally. "Let's just say that I did want to attract Ian's attention—this is purely hypothetical, of course. How do you think I could do it?"

"Well, you could start by wearing more gray. And Ian likes geometric patterns, especially squares. And perhaps you could find something with letters and numbers printed on it."

It suddenly dawned on Victoria what Sally was getting at. "You mean dress like a computer keyboard?"

"That's the only way you'll ever get him to put his hands on you!" Sally said, laughing. She gathered up her stuff and started toward the school steps.

"Thanks," Victoria called after her sarcastically. "Thanks for nothing."

Katia and John were sitting on the lawn, talking with Deb, when they saw Nikki. She was walking toward them across the leaf-strewn front lawn, waving happily. She stopped to talk to a few people she knew and said hello to several more before finally making it over to them.

"Welcome back to the land of the living," John said, wrapping his arm around her shoulder.

"Oh, come on, I was never dead," Nikki said. "I just didn't feel too good for a few hours there."

"How's your cut?" Katia asked.

Nikki patted the gauze bandage on her face. "I know everyone's going to be asking me all day what's wrong with my face and making a lot of bad jokes. I can't wait to hear what Sally has to say about it. Actually, it's a lot better now. The swelling's gone down, and I'll only have to wear the bandage a couple more days."

"That's good," Katia said. "But don't worry about people bugging you—everyone's already heard the whole story. It's all anyone's talking about."

"And if anyone tries to make fun of you, just send them to me," John told her.

"Or me," Deb said. "I'll belt them." She made a boxing motion with her fist. "Uppercut, just like that. They won't know what hit them."

"Unless they're over five feet four," John teased. "That's about as far as you can reach."

"Hey, it's not my fault I'm short," Deb said, pretending to be hurt. She looked around. "Anyone seen Suzanne? I called her last night, but her mom said she'd gone to bed early."

"She did have a pretty tiring day," said Katia.

"That's an understatement," John added.

Nikki smiled. "Well, I hope no one has any big plans for the weekend, because I've decided to throw a party Friday night—in Suzanne's honor. I mean, if it weren't for Suzanne, I might not be here right now."

Victoria had come up to the group while Nikki was talking about Suzanne, and Katia could tell from the look on her face that she definitely was not pleased.

"And if it weren't for Suzanne, you wouldn't have run away into the woods and slipped and fallen into the river in the first place," Victoria said. "Did you happen to mention that to everyone?"

"Maybe seeing her did upset me," Nikki said, turning to Victoria with a puzzled expression. "But that has nothing to do with what happened or what she did afterward."

"Hey, Victoria, is that new?" John reached over and pointed at the diamond bracelet dangling from her slender wrist.

"That's gorgeous," Deb said. "Wow. In fact, it's incredible. When did you get it?"

"My father gave it to me this morning," Victoria said. "I guess he was just so glad I was okay. He said he got really scared when he thought maybe I was the one who'd fallen into the river."

John gave Victoria a skeptical glance. "Really?"

"I need a father like that," Katia joked.

"No, you don't," Victoria said, a sad, almost soulful tone in her voice. "Trust me." She smiled faintly.

Katia smiled. "I think I know what you mean, but it's still a beautiful bracelet." She turned to John. He was gazing at Victoria, as if he was trying to figure out something about her. Katia tugged at his sleeve. "Let's go hit our lockers before first bell, okay?"

"Sure," John said.

Katia wondered what kind of silent communication was going on between John and Victoria. She remembered what Deb had told her the last time Katia had complained about John and Victoria's strange, close friendship: "They had such an intense relationship," Deb had said. "Of course they know each other really well. It doesn't mean they're anything but close friends."

And that's the way it's going to stay, Katia told herself as she and John walked up the rest of the steps and into the school. The two of them belonged together now. And nothing—especially not Victoria Hill—would tear them apart.

"I don't know if you heard me before," Nikki said to Victoria after John and Katia had left. "But I was just telling everyone that I'm having a party Friday. For Suzanne."

Victoria looked at Nikki, then at Deb, then back at Nikki. "You're kidding, right?"

"No. Why would I be kidding?" Nikki asked. "Suzanne saved my life yesterday, remember?"

"Yeah, and Suzanne tried to steal your boyfriend the day before. Remember?" Victoria shook her head. "Jeez, Nikki, do I have to hold up a sign for you every time you're around Suzanne? This girl means trouble."

"Victoria," Deb warned, "don't get into that. Nikki's already forgiven her, and so should you. Suzanne made a mistake, she apologized—end of story."

"A *mistake?* I'll say. End of story? I sincerely doubt that. And I can't believe you're buying that from her," Victoria scoffed.

"It's not a question of buying it," Nikki said. "I believe her."

"Well, I don't," Victoria said. "First she comes waltzing into town from Brooklyn of all places, with some sob story about how her dad died before she was born, boo-hoo, and we're all supposed to feel *so* sorry for her. Then it turns out that what she said wasn't true at all." Victoria paused. "Nikki, we don't know the slightest thing about Suzanne yet. For all we know, that's the first of many things she's lied to us about, and—"

"First of all, she didn't lie to us on purpose. She didn't know about her father!" Nikki protested.

"Well, then, what else doesn't she know? I mean, maybe she has some dark, secret past, and no one really knows who she is."

"Give her a break!" Deb snapped. "So what if she doesn't know her father? That doesn't make her a bad person, Victoria, and that doesn't mean she has a secret past. You think everyone who doesn't know their birth parents has some horrible, dirty secret? Maybe you've forgotten, but I don't know who my birth parents are—I'm adopted, remember?"

Victoria stared at her. "Good grief, I didn't mean you, Deb. We all know that whoever your birth parents are, you're about as normal as they come. I wasn't implying that you had any secrets in your past. In fact, I bet your birth parents are as sunny and cheerful as you—"

"Stop it!" Deb cried. She grabbed her knapsack from the concrete steps and took off through the crowd.

"What's eating her?" Victoria asked.

"You can't assume things about Deb's biological parents," Nikki said. "I'm sure she's just as afraid to find out who they are as Suzanne is shocked to find out her father is still alive. It must be hard to be adopted and hear everyone talking about fathers and mothers."

"Well, personally, I'd be happy if I had parents as nice as Deb's, even if they aren't her quote unquote real parents," Victoria said. "If I were her, I'd be happy with what I had."

Nikki shrugged. "Maybe. But maybe you'd want to know more about where you came from, too."

"Who knows? I might," Victoria said. "But there's something much more important I've been wanting to ask you. How are things between you and Luke, anyway, since Suzanne decided to make a move on him?"

"A little weird, but mostly okay," Nikki said. "I think what happened yesterday made us both wake up. I mean, maybe we *are* having some problems, and maybe we *don't* always understand each other, but we do really love each other."

"Mmm." Victoria shrugged. "Then I guess things are back to normal. I bet Suzanne's bummed. She really has a thing for him, but I assume you've noticed."

"Victoria, Suzanne said that kiss was a mistake, and considering what she did for me yesterday, I'd like to believe her," Nikki said. "Especially since Luke's apologized about a million times, too. Now, can we close this topic once and for all?"

"If you want to believe her, go right ahead," Victoria said dismissively. "Just don't expect me to agree with you."

Nikki didn't know why Victoria was so set against Suzanne. *Maybe she's just trying to protect me. After all, she is my best friend,* Nikki thought as the first bell rang and she picked up her books to head into school. Still, she knew she could trust Suzanne from now on.

The only person she wasn't sure she could completely trust again was Luke. He still needed to prove himself to her.

There he is. Suzanne's stomach did flip-flops when she spotted Luke standing in front of his locker, talking with Keith and John. He was wearing his usual: a black T-shirt, worn jeans, and motorcycle boots. She'd told herself a dozen times not to get worked up over seeing him, that it wasn't a big deal. But whenever she was around Luke, even standing half-way down the hallway from him, Suzanne lost track of everything else. All she could think about was how good it had felt to kiss him Saturday night, how she had wanted that moment never to end—

Snap out of it, she told herself. *This isn't getting you anywhere.* Thinking about Luke that way would only make her miserable. Suzanne shifted her book bag on her shoulder. She'd made up her mind that she needed to say something to Luke, just to clear the air, so that they weren't always so awkward with each other, especially when Nikki was around. She was Nikki's true friend now. Whatever feelings she had for Luke would have to be ignored.

Suzanne glanced at her watch. The bell for third period was about to ring. She couldn't put this off any longer—she had to talk to Luke. But Keith and John were still hanging out by his locker. She could hardly go up to the three of them and tell Luke she wanted to talk to him alone.

Finally! she thought as Keith and John walked away. She took a deep breath and went over to Luke. This was going to take every ounce of strength and courage she had. *Come on,* she told herself. *You pulled someone out of a raging river yesterday. You can handle one small conversation.*

"Hi," she said, stopping in front of him.

He turned at the sound of her voice, and seemed surprised to see her. "Suzanne. Um . . . what's up?"

"I just have something I need to tell you," Suzanne began. That standing next to you makes my knees go weak. That our kiss the other night was the most passionate moment of my entire life.

"Shoot," Luke said with a casual shrug, but he looked nervous, as though he was afraid of what she might say.

"The other night on the golf course—what happened between us—it was a big mistake," Suzanne said quickly. "I know that now. I know you and Nikki have something special together, and I don't want to get in the way."

"Suzanne," Luke began, "I know. I mean, I shouldn't have taken advantage of the situation. I didn't mean to hurt you or anything. I just—"

"No, it's okay." Suzanne struggled to keep the emotion out of her voice. She didn't want Luke to know how she really felt inside, which was the exact opposite of what she was trying to say. "It was just that I wasn't thinking straight. I was upset that night when I bumped into you. I felt lonely, and you happened to be there. That's all. Look, I'll see you later, okay?" Suzanne tried to smile at Luke, but she felt as if she were about to explode. She had to get away from him. She hurried off down the hall and ducked into the girls' room just as the bell rang. She locked herself in a stall, rested her head against the metal partition, and burst out crying.

All day everyone had been talking about how wonderful she was, how brave she was, how she was Hillcrest's hero. She'd heard it so many times, it made her want to throw up.

Some superhero. Wonder Woman wouldn't cry over some boy she'd kissed once. A boy who'd decided he'd rather stay with his long-term girlfriend.

She'd been crazy to think that Luke really cared about her. He was in love with Nikki, Nikki was in love with him, and Suzanne didn't belong in the picture anywhere, except as Nikki's friend. Suzanne knew she ought to be grateful that Nikki had forgiven her, but at the moment she didn't feel grateful at all. She felt as if she'd just given up the most important thing in her life—for nothing.

Nine

"Here's a towel. Thanks again," Suzanne said to Mrs. Grayce at Willis Workout late Monday afternoon. "Have a great workout!"

Mrs. Grayce was a regular, one of the many members who came to work out on their way home from the office. The fitness studio was always packed from five o'clock until about seven-thirty, and Suzanne helped out at the front desk or wherever she was needed most during those hours.

The phone on the front desk beeped, and Suzanne lifted the handset. "Yes?"

"Suzanne, could you bring some extra towels into the women's locker room?" her mother asked. "I'm in here, and the bin is empty."

"Sure." Suzanne hung up the phone and grabbed a bunch of towels from the stack the laundry service had just delivered. "I'll be back in a second—can you keep an eye on the desk?" she asked Geoff, one of the trainers.

"Sure thing," Geoff said. "But hurry back—I've got to go to the weight room soon."

Suzanne walked quickly through the studio toward the back and opened the door to the women's locker room. She walked right past her mother, who was fixing her hair in front of a mirror. "Here you go." She put the towels into the bin by the shower stalls.

"Thanks, hon. So how's it going?" Ms. Willis asked. "Anything new at school?"

"I have to get back to the front desk," Suzanne said without making eye contact.

"Suzanne, are you going to avoid me forever?" Ms. Willis asked, following her daughter to the locker room door.

Suzanne turned around and faced her, arms folded across her chest. "Mom, you lied to me about something really important. I mean, I'm not going to just get over this." Suzanne paused. "I'm, uh, thinking about finding Steven Carew."

Ms. Willis looked stunned. "Are you sure that's a good idea?"

"No," Suzanne said brusquely. She knew that what she was about to say would hurt her mother deeply, but she continued anyway. "I'm *not* sure. In fact, I'm not sure about much of anything anymore. I feel like my whole life's changed, like all the rules have been changed, only someone forgot to tell me what they were."

"I'm sorry, I really am," Suzanne's mother said. "If there were any way I could take back all those years and . . . and have told you the truth from the beginning, I would. But I can't."

"And you can't tell me any more about him, is that right?" Suzanne asked, stepping aside as a woman came into the locker room. "Because you haven't seen him in all this time."

Ms. Willis nodded. "I'm sorry. He just doesn't want anything to do with either one of us, honey."

"How do you know that?" Suzanne said defensively. "He might want to know me, but he doesn't even know I exist—isn't that what you told me?"

"Yes, that's what I told you," her mother said. "And that's the truth."

"Really? The *truth*. What a concept." Suzanne rolled her eyes. "Look, I have to get back to the desk, or else Geoff's going to kill me."

She yanked open the door and headed back toward the front of the studio. The way Suzanne was feeling, she didn't want to talk to her mother about her father—or about anything. She didn't want to deal with somebody who'd lied to her, even if it was supposed to have been for her own good.

Besides, if her mother could keep something that big a secret for so long, Suzanne wondered what other secrets she could have been keeping from her.

Keith walked down Oak Street Monday night, whistling, heading for the weekly poker game. It was a new week, and he was ready to take his weekend winnings and turn them into more. It was going to be a great night—he just had a feeling.

This is exactly what I need to get my mind off everything else, he thought. So what if Nikki barely even acknowledged me at school today, after all that intense stuff at the bowling alley Saturday night? At least I thought it was intense.

So what if Luke paid me about the same amount of attention—none? He should have been grateful to me for not moving in on Nikki, Keith thought, and shook his head. Luke had been acting strange and distant lately—more so than usual. It was as though Luke had too much on his mind to deal with anyone else. Anyone except Nikki, anyway. Keith couldn't say he blamed him. If he were dating Nikki, he wouldn't want to spend time with anyone else, either.

And then there was that wild story about Suzanne Willis coming to Nikki's rescue.

Maybe I ought to give Suzanne another look, Keith mused as he knocked at the side door of Mr. Martin's house, the door that led straight to the basement and the secret poker game.

"Back for more?" Mr. Martin asked, opening the door.

"You bet," Keith said. "No pun intended."

"Hey, we'll be glad to see you bet as much as you want," Mr. Martin said as Keith followed him downstairs to the basement. "We're playing with ones, fives, and tens. Need to make any change from the bank of Martin?"

Keith shook his head. "No, thanks. Hi, everybody, how's it going?"

"We saved a place for you," Mr. Hammersmith said, gesturing to an empty chair.

Sally Ross's father smiled. "Hello, Keith."

Mr. Palmer nodded. "This chair's got your name on it, buddy."

"Yeah, we had a feeling you'd be back," Mr. Lopez said. "After that lucky run you had Saturday night, we figured you might want to try again."

"Of course I'm back," Keith said, straddling the metal folding chair. The chair's legs scraped loudly against the concrete floor as he scooted closer to the table. "I'm thinking about doubling my money this time."

He saw Mr. Martin exchange a look with Mr. Hammersmith.

"Sure, Keith. Whatever you say," Mr. Hammersmith said, adjusting his glasses. "We're happy to take your money anytime. Day, night, weekend, weekday . . . Heck, you can even call us in the middle of the night and we'll get a game together for you."

The other guys at the table laughed, and Keith smiled. If that was what they thought was going to happen, they had another thing coming. He wasn't about to lose any of his money. He tossed a dollar into the ante pool, and Mr. Martin dealt the first hand of five-card draw.

Keith picked up his cards. He couldn't believe it. Five hearts. He had a royal flush. One of the best hands in poker. When the betting started, he tossed a few tens into the pot. "I'll see your ten, and raise you twenty," he said to Mr. Hammersmith, who'd started the betting.

"Whoa. That's a lot of money," Mr. Ross said.

"Hey, you know what they say—it takes money to make money," Keith said with a shrug.

"Don't I know it. On my salary, I'm lucky if I have enough left over even to show up here with a couple of bucks," Mr. Lopez said. "I've got to turn it into more or it's going to be a blue Christmas at my house."

Keith felt bad for a second, but then he

said to himself, He's just saying that so I'll feel sorry for him and stop winning. But that's not going to happen. I'm nice and all, but I'm not a sucker.

"Cards, Keith?" Mr. Martin asked.

Keith shook his head. "No, thanks."

"Uh-oh." Mr. Hammersmith slid three cards across the table to Mr. Martin. "I'll take three."

He has a pair and that's it, Keith thought, watching the rest of the men exchange their cards. I've got it made, from the looks of things. He smiled as the betting began again, and he matched Mr. Hammersmith's twenty-dollar bet.

"What do you have?" Keith asked.

Mr. Hammersmith laid down his cards. "Three of a kind."

Keith fanned his cards out and put them on the table. "Royal flush."

"That beats me," Mr. Lopez said.

"Me too," Mr. Palmer chimed in.

Keith grabbed the heap of cash on the table and pulled it toward him. "Looks like another great night for yours truly."

"The night is young," Mr. Hammersmith said. "We haven't even gotten started yet."

Maybe not, but talk about starting off on the right foot, Keith thought, tossing a dollar into the ante pool for the next hand. Make that the right hand. He smiled and picked up his cards.

Suzanne walked out of school Tuesday afternoon and started down the stairs toward the bike rack. It was sunny and warm outside, and she wasn't too psyched about spending another afternoon inside at her mother's workout studio. But she didn't have much choice. Her mother was still looking for people to fill all the positions at the gym, and Suzanne could use the extra money she made.

Suzanne bent down beside her mountain bike and turned the key in her lock. When she stood up, she saw Luke and Nikki standing in front of the buses lined up to take students home.

Luke had his arms around Nikki's waist, and he was smiling at her. Suzanne couldn't remember ever seeing him with such a big smile before—Luke tended to be on the gloomy side at times. But now he looked like the happiest guy in the world.

Of course he is. He messed up, and Nikki took him back, Suzanne thought. He's probably so grateful he got away with it that he won't stop smiling for a week. Because even if his intentions were good, Suzanne knew, Luke *had* gotten away with something. He'd kissed her, and Nikki had taken him back anyway. And now that it was all over, Suzanne couldn't help feeling angry. She was the one who'd ended up with nothing. Luke and Nikki still had each other. They hadn't lost anything.

Suzanne got onto her bicycle and, after slinging her book bag across her back, started riding past them.

"Suzanne, wait up!"

She turned and saw Nikki waving to her. Luke was walking away across the lawn on the side of the school. Suzanne slowed down and made a U-turn, circling back to where Nikki stood on the sidewalk.

"Hey, what's up?" she said casually, coasting to a stop.

"Were you just about to ride by without saying hello, or was that my imagination?" Nikki asked.

"Oh—I didn't see you," Suzanne lied. "You know how it is after school. All I can think about is getting out of here."

"Some days I definitely feel that way," Nikki said. "Well, anyway, I'm glad I ran into you—I was going to call you later. I want to have a party Friday night."

"Sounds like fun," Suzanne said, shrugging. "Do you want me to help you plan it or set up or anything?"

"You can't lift a finger, actually," Nikki said.

"This isn't just any old Friday-night party. It's a party in honor of you."

Suzanne's eyes widened, and she felt a flutter of excitement. "Me?"

"Yes, you," Nikki said. "Of course you. You only jumped into a river to drag me out. The least I can do is put some chips in a bowl and invite a bunch of people over."

Suzanne laughed. "Chips? Is that all?" She pretended to be offended. "Don't I even rate salsa?"

"Actually, it's going to be a megablast!" Nikki said. "In fact, since you haven't been to a party at my house before, I'm going to make it totally amazing. You know, we haven't had a party since the school year started. This could be the blowout everyone talks about for the rest of the year."

"Oh, I get it," Suzanne teased. "It's kind of for me, but it's kind of for your reputation as hostess extraordinaire, too, right?"

"Right," Nikki said, laughing. "Anyway, it'll give you a chance to meet and talk to some people you probably don't know yet."

"A Welcome Wagon kind of thing," Suzanne said with a grin. "Yeah, somebody in Brooklyn warned me about those. I don't have to buy any plastic bowls, do I?"

Nikki hit Suzanne on the arm with her purse. "Will you quit kidding around? I'm serious,

Suzanne. You deserve a party, so I'm having one."

"Well, okay. Thanks," Suzanne said. "Sounds great." She couldn't believe Nikki wanted to throw a party in her honor, but she certainly wasn't going to talk her out of it.

Maybe Hillcrest was going to start feeling like home after all, she thought as she slowly pedaled down the street beside Nikki. *I wonder if Luke will be at the party?* she thought before she could stop herself.

Of course he would—as Nikki's date. And Suzanne would have to live with that, as hard as that seemed at the moment. She'd just act natural—but what's natural when you're in love with your best friend's boyfriend?

Ten

"Dude, you wouldn't even believe it if I told you how much I made last night." Keith looked through the CDs on the front counter at the Tunesmith. Luke was working that afternoon, and Keith had come downtown as soon as football practice ended to hang out and kill some time before going home for dinner. "You totally wouldn't believe how much."

"So don't tell me, then, and I won't have to try," Luke said.

"Sounds like you're a little jealous, man," Keith said.

"Actually, I'm glad somebody around here has some money," Luke grumbled.

"Things are rough, huh?" Keith said, and Luke nodded. Luke had problems at home that Keith could barely even imagine, never mind deal with as well as Luke had. "How's your mom?"

"Don't ask," Luke replied morosely. Luke's mother was an alcoholic. She'd just lost her latest job and was making no effort to find another one. Their rent was already overdue. "I might as well start working here full-time, only I'd have to drop out of school," Luke said, shaking his head.

"You wouldn't do that, would you?" Keith asked.

"No, I guess not. But it sure would make things easier," Luke said. "Hey, take off for a second—Rick's coming." Luke started nervously arranging the pens in the cup by the register, knocking the cup over and scrambling to get everything on the counter looking neat and orderly before his boss saw him goofing off.

Keith went to the New Releases section and started browsing while Luke talked with Rick. *Luke sure seems wound up about something,* Keith thought, picking up a new disc and glancing at the song titles. Keith had noticed Luke's hands shaking when Rick approached the desk.

A few minutes later, Luke found Keith looking through the jazz CDs. "I have my break now—want to grab something to eat?" Luke asked.

"Sure. I'll buy you a cone," Keith offered as they headed outside to the ice cream parlor just down the block.

"You'd *better* be buying," Luke said, laughing. "And make it a double sundae. What good is all that money if you can't spend it on your friends?"

"Exactly," Keith said. "You know what? After another game like last night's, I'll be able to spend a lot on everyone. Maybe even buy new equipment for our band, new amps or something."

"You're pretty sure of yourself, aren't you?" Luke asked as they walked into the ice cream parlor.

"What can I say? I'm a poker guru," Keith said. "I slammed those dudes so hard last night, it was unbelievable. On every hand I either won or folded before I lost any serious money. They didn't know what hit them. I even convinced them to play again tonight."

"So what are you waiting for? Call the airlines and get on the first flight to Vegas. I'm sure they're waiting for you at one of the big casinos—probably saving you a seat, just wondering when the great Keith Stein is going to show up," Luke teased him. "The chips are getting cold while you sit around in Hillcrest with a bunch of amateurs."

Keith laughed. "Sorry. I guess I *have* been

kind of obnoxious. But the thing is, I'm so hyper about tonight that I can't do anything else, can't talk about anything else."

"What are you saying? You're playing poker again tonight too?" Luke asked. "Why don't you just take what you've already won and run? Consider yourself lucky."

"It's not about luck!" Keith was offended. "How many times do I have to tell people that? I mean, if I only won once or twice and then had a bad night, okay. *That* would be luck. But I'm on a roll, man."

"Sure it isn't just a lucky roll?" Luke asked as he stepped up to the counter to order. "Everyone has streaks, you know. And luck eventually runs out. Besides, aren't some of those guys you play with practically professional gamblers?"

"Nah." Keith shook his head. "They like to think they're better than me, but I've beaten them so many times now, they know they're dealing with someone as good as they are. Luke, it's not like I haven't done my homework. I was reading this book about poker all weekend—odds, hands, strategies. I know what I'm doing. You know, if you want, I could get you in on a game one of these nights."

"So you can clean me out, too? No, thanks," Luke said. "I think I'll hold on to the small amount I do have."

Keith nodded and ordered a large waffle cone with chocolate-chip ice cream. As much as he liked to gamble, he could understand why Luke wouldn't. Maybe if things keep going the way they have been, I'll be able to loan Luke some money, help him and his mother out, he thought.

And if things kept going as well as they had been, he was going to have plenty of money left over to do whatever he wanted.

Luke slowly walked back to the Tunesmith after his ice cream break with Keith. He almost dreaded going back, knowing he'd have to sock away some more money before the day was out. Luke wasn't proud of the fact that he'd been stealing from his boss—pocketing the money customers paid for CDs instead of ringing them up on the register—but he didn't really have a choice. If he didn't get the rent money to the landlord soon, he and his mother would be out on the street. Somehow he couldn't imagine Nikki dating a homeless guy.

"Hey, you're back just in time." Luke's coworker, Mark, was behind the register. "I have to unload some major boxes out back. Can you handle the action in here by yourself?"

"Sure, no prob, man," Luke answered. "Where's Rick?"

"Out and about," Mark said on his way to the back door.

Luke was relieved to be on his own in the store. He could siphon off some cash without worrying about Mark or Rick catching him.

The bell on the front door jangled as a fortysomething man walked in. "Do you have any Roy Buchanan?" the man asked.

"Yeah, it's over in the blues section," Luke said. "They're in alphabetical order."

A couple of minutes later the man brought a two-CD collection up to the register. "That'll be thirty-one dollars with tax," Luke said, calculating the amount in his head and rounding it off to the nearest dollar.

The man gave him a twenty, a ten, and a one. Luke paused a moment, looking around the store to make sure the coast was clear. Then he used the key to open the register so he didn't have to ring up the sale. He carefully put the money under the cash drawer, and when the man left, Luke transferred the bills to his pocket, his heart pounding in his chest. He took a deep breath.

This has got to be the last time. I can't take the pressure much longer.

Victoria was walking down the third-floor hall on her way to English class Wednesday morning when she saw John and Katia standing by the water fountain, kissing. *Why does everyone in this entire school have a relationship except me?* she thought as she spotted another couple locked in a passionate embrace just past John and Katia. It was enough to make her want to transfer to another school.

"Hey, lovebirds," Victoria said, stopping in front of John and Katia. She tapped John on the shoulder. "Sorry to break up the party, but we do have class in a couple of minutes."

John slowly turned around, releasing Katia's waist. "We do?"

Katia giggled. "I almost forgot we were in school."

"Yeah, yeah." Victoria sighed. "Wish I could say the same, but then, I'm not in love and spending my time between classes swapping spit."

"Hey, give us a break," John said, laughing.

"John, I'll see you after school—before practice, okay? Just a quick hello before Coach gets to work your cute butt off," Katia said, pausing in the doorway to the classroom.

John nodded. "Have a great algebra class."

"Gee, thanks." Katia made a face at him, then walked into the room.

Victoria and John walked down the hall to the English class they had together.

"So how's it been going?" John asked.

"Okay." She shrugged. "Not great." She wasn't going to bore John with the pathetic details of her own miserable love life. "What about you? You look pretty happy these days."

"Yeah, I guess I am," John said, bumping against Victoria as a group of boys passed by.

"How are things working out with you and Katia?" Victoria asked.

"Pretty good," John said.

Victoria sighed. "I wish I could find someone who made me that happy. I mean, it seems as though ever since we broke up, I've had rotten luck with guys. Am I really so awful to go out with?"

"Get real," John said, shaking his head. "Ian Houghton's got about as much sense as a cactus. Any guy who'd diss you on a date doesn't deserve even to talk to you again."

"So you heard about that? News sure does travel fast around here." Victoria didn't know whether to be glad that John still cared about her or humiliated that he knew about her comatose romantic life. "The whole thing makes me feel like I never want to go out with anyone again. But I hate to just give up. Ian may be a jerk, but he *is* pretty cute."

"Yeah, for an idiot," John said. "And what's this about not going out with anyone ever again? Come on, Victoria, things can't be that bad. You know you're still the hottest girl at Hillcrest . . . except for Katia, of course."

Except for Katia, Victoria thought as she took her seat in the second row of the class, right behind John. She stared at his muscular back, the way his shoulders looked rock solid under his shirt, the slight curl of his dark brown hair.

If it weren't for Katia, Victoria thought, I'd probably make a move on John right now. The way she was feeling, she could easily picture throwing herself into John's embrace. She remembered all the times they'd tried to break up, only to get back together because they ended up in each other's arms at the end of a party or after a football game. When Victoria was with John, sparks flew—no doubt about it.

But the sparks had flown too fast and furiously when Victoria caught John seeing another girl on the side, and she'd broken up with him—for good.

But all of a sudden her decision seemed to be the wrong one. She hadn't realized at the time how tough it would be for her to find another guy who turned her on even half as much as John did. And it wasn't just a physical thing, either. She and John had always understood each other, even though on the surface they seemed to have so little in common. John was the person she confided in, the only person except Nikki who knew the real Victoria. Why had she thrown that away?

Because John was unfaithful to me, she reminded herself as the bell rang. And he'd probably do it again if he got the chance.

She'd just have to find a new guy—somebody who'd understand her as well as John had, but who wouldn't cheat on her. It might take a little while, but she could wait.

At least a few more days, anyway. Until Nikki's party. She knew Ian would be there—nobody ever dared *not* show up at the Stewarts', not for one of the biggest parties of the year . . . even if its theme was a little lame. She hoped Nikki wasn't going to make too big a deal out of this party-in-honor-of stuff.

With my luck, Ian will probably end up liking Suzanne, she thought, doodling Ian's name in her notebook.

She could see it now. Ian would probably ditch the party and go into the den to work on the Stewarts' computer. He'd be hunched over the keyboard, typing messages to his friends on the Internet. He'd be concentrating so intensely that he wouldn't notice Victoria come into the room. She'd walk up behind him, put her hands over his eyes, and whisper, "Guess who?"

When he realized it was her, he'd pull her around to face him. Victoria would push the computer away and sit down, and then she'd kiss him so passionately he'd never want to log on to the Internet again. . . .

Eleven

Nikki dabbed at her temples with a white towel that had a large red WW monogram embroidered on it. "Wow. That class was harder than I expected." She, Deb, and Victoria had gone to Willis Workout after school Wednesday for the advanced step aerobics class. Now they were headed for the juice bar, where Suzanne had said she'd meet them after running a few errands for her mother.

"No kidding," Deb said. "I think I'll try the intermediate level next time."

"Not me." Victoria sat on a stool at the bar. "I love intense workouts. That way I get to sweat out all the rotten things that happened during the day and start over." She wiped the back of her neck with a towel. "Besides, it does wonders for the complexion.

Speaking of which, yours looks great, Nikki."

"Yeah, that cut on your face is healing pretty well," Deb said, sitting beside Victoria. "Just in time for the big party Friday night."

"I can't wait," Nikki said. "It's going to be so great. I've got some terrific ideas for decorating the house."

"I can make some nachos or something," Deb offered. "Or maybe something fancier."

Victoria rolled her eyes. "It's just a stupid party. Stop acting like there are going to be movie stars showing up."

"You mean they're not? Oh, no," Deb gasped, grasping the bar. "I'm so disappointed."

Nikki laughed. She loved watching Deb and Victoria go at it, as long as she knew they weren't seriously arguing.

"All I meant was, it seems like *some* people are getting a little carried away." Victoria arched one eyebrow as Suzanne approached the three of them, then leaned forward and propped her elbows on the bar. "Excuse me? Could we have a little service down here?" Victoria snapped her fingers impatiently. "*Hello!*" she said in an annoyed voice, but the bartender didn't turn around.

Suzanne walked up to the bar and stood beside Victoria. "Tim?" she called to the man tending bar. "When you get a chance, can we please have some mineral waters and— What else do you guys want?" She turned to the group.

"Freshly squeezed grapefruit juice," Victoria said. "If you have it."

"Sure thing." Tim smiled and poured some into a glass. "There you go. Be careful, it's very tart."

"Don't worry, I think she can handle it," Suzanne said, sliding it toward Victoria with a small smile. "Thanks, Tim."

"Could I just be really boring and have a diet soda?" Deb asked.

"You could, but how about trying our special drink? It's called Nutrient Blast. It'll replace all the stuff you just used up," Tim suggested. "It tastes like fresh cherries."

"Okay," Deb said with a shrug. "If it'll bring me back to life, I'm game." She took the glass Tim handed her.

"So how was the class?" Suzanne asked, pulling a stool across the floor from one of the tables. She perched beside Nikki.

"Great," Nikki said, sipping her mineral water.

"A little too easy, if you ask me," Victoria said, sounding bored. She sipped her grapefruit juice through a tiny straw. "Maybe your mother ought to consider adding a class for the really advanced. At this club in Manhattan I've been to, they have Extreme Aerobics."

"I've heard of that," Suzanne said. "I'll

suggest it. Only that means I'll have to talk to my mother, which I don't plan on doing anytime soon."

"Uh-oh," Deb said. "That doesn't sound good."

"Are you still mad at her?" Nikki asked sympathetically. "Did she say anything else about your father?"

Suzanne shook her head, tying a double knot in the laces of one of her cross-training shoes. "No, she didn't say anything else about him, and yeah, I'm still angry. I don't know if I'll ever be able to forgive her. She keeps trying to explain why she kept the whole thing a secret for all these years, but after a while, there really isn't much to say."

"Except she could tell you who he is," Victoria said. "That's really the least she could do, considering how she lied to you. Aren't you dying to find him?"

"I already know who he is, sort of," Suzanne said. "I mean, I know his name. I just don't know where to find him. He disappeared."

"Off the face of the earth?" Victoria scoffed. "I doubt that."

"I can't imagine knowing who my father was," Deb said. "Even his name. It would be too weird."

"Yeah, that's a lot to deal with," Nikki said. "Is your mother going to help you find him, Suzanne?"

"I'd doubt that," Victoria said.

"What makes you say that?" Suzanne asked in a challenging tone.

"Please don't argue, you guys," Nikki began.

"No, I want to know why you said that," Suzanne insisted, glaring at Victoria.

"I said it because she's obviously holding back certain information." Victoria gave Suzanne a long look.

"And what makes you think my mother's holding back information?"

Victoria stirred the juice with her straw. "There's something I don't get. How can you *not* be able to find someone? You look around yourself for a little while, use your own resources, and when that doesn't work, you hire a private detective, and *voilà*. You find your man. It happens all the time."

"Maybe my mother didn't have the money to hire a private detective," Suzanne argued. "Did you ever think of that? She was only working as a waitress at the time he disappeared."

"Okay. Let's assume she didn't have the money back then. But she certainly does now," Victoria said, tossing the straw onto the bar. "Look around this place. It had to cost big bucks."

"She took out a loan—a business loan,"

Suzanne said. "Anyway, she has a partner, a silent partner. It's not like she bought this place by herself."

"Even so," Victoria said, "if she wanted to find him, for your sake, she could have."

"Since you've given the whole situation so much thought, let me ask you—why *wouldn't* she want to find him? I know what she says about that, but what do you say?" Suzanne asked.

Nikki was starting to feel very uncomfortable. Wasn't this Suzanne's private, personal life? Why were they all talking about it as if it were a jigsaw puzzle?

"He's obviously somebody she's ashamed of, for whatever reason," Victoria said, "and she doesn't want to bring him back into her life. Maybe his life is a mess, maybe he was a criminal—"

"Victoria, you're getting a little carried away," Nikki warned.

"Try a *lot* carried away," Deb added.

"Of course, if you're afraid of the truth . . ." Victoria paused.

"I'm not *afraid* of anything," Suzanne retorted.

"Good," Victoria said. "Then why don't you ask your mother to hire a detective? And if she won't, I'll lend you the money to hire one. That way you'll know the answer to this mystery and you can get on with your life."

Suzanne didn't answer right away. Nikki knew that if Victoria lent Suzanne money, it wouldn't be to ease Suzanne's mind—it would be to satisfy Victoria's own curiosity. She wanted to find some dirt on Suzanne, and this was the way she meant to do it.

"You don't have to do anything right away," Nikki said, placing her hand on Suzanne's arm.

"Yeah, there's no rush," Deb added with a sideways glance at Victoria. "And whatever you decide to do, we're all behind you. Right?"

"Definitely," Nikki said.

"Like I already told you, I'll help any way I can," Victoria said, her lips in a scheming smile.

"Table for two? Where's Patricia tonight?" Victoria asked her mother as they sat at the dining room table Wednesday night, eating a light dinner of soup and salad. Victoria had felt so great after her hard workout that afternoon, the last thing she wanted was to eat a big, heavy meal.

"Your sister's at a pizza party for her soccer club," Mrs. Hill said.

"What about Daddy? Where's he off to?"

"He has a dinner engagement," Mrs. Hill replied. "Something down at the Rotary Club."

"Don't tell me. The mayor again?" Victoria sighed.

"Beats me. He has so many social plans lately," her mother said. "He's either at the Elks, the Lions, or the country club, or there's something at work . . . I can't keep track of his schedule anymore." She paused, and Victoria suddenly felt a wave of sympathy for her mother.

"So how was school today?" Mrs. Hill asked, passing a bottle of lemon vinaigrette dressing to Victoria.

"Same as usual, Mom," Victoria said, drizzling a few drops of dressing onto the spinach leaves on her plate.

"And how are you getting along with that new girl . . . what's her name? The one who pulled Nikki out of the river." Mrs. Hill sipped from her glass of wine.

"She and I get along just fine," Victoria lied. "Would you please pass the breadsticks, Mom?"

Victoria heard her father coming down the stairs, and a few moments later Mr. Hill stood in the doorway. "Sorry to skip out on you two. I've had more than enough of rubbing elbows with politicians this week, but business is business. I'll probably get in late, so I'll see you two tomorrow morning." He walked over and kissed Victoria on the cheek. "Good night, Victoria."

The smell of liquor on his breath was so strong that Victoria cringed. She could see it now—her father would be pulled over for DUI. Lately the local newspaper had started printing the names and photographs of people who were arrested for drunk driving. It was supposed to motivate people to stop. The last thing she needed was her father's picture in the paper. She'd die of embarrassment! It was bad enough that half the kids at school already knew he was a drunk, from the time he'd crashed her big party last spring, totally plastered and acting like a complete jerk.

"Daddy, how about if I drop you off at your dinner?" she suggested. "I'm almost done eating. It'll be fun—we can talk on the way."

"Victoria, your father's perfectly capable of getting downtown himself. And since when are you so helpful?" Mrs. Hill asked.

"Really, it's no problem," Victoria insisted, tossing her linen napkin onto the table. "I was . . . going to Nikki's anyway, to study, and it's practically on the way. When you're done with your meeting, I'm sure one of the people there could give you a ride home."

"I'll drive myself, Victoria," Mr. Hill said, glaring at her. "And that's the end of this discussion." He straightened his tie and walked out of the dining room. A minute later Victoria heard the garage door open, followed by the purr of her father's Jaguar.

"What was that all about?" Victoria's

mother asked. "Are you really in such a hurry to get to Nikki's house?"

"Mom, we can't let Dad keep doing what he's doing," Victoria said.

"What are you talking about?"

Daddy knows what I'm talking about—that's why he got so testy all of a sudden. Can Mom really be so oblivious? "Mom, Daddy's been drinking tonight," Victoria said.

"He had a drink before he left the house. What's the big deal about that? I'm enjoying a glass of wine with dinner," her mother said. "Your father likes to have a drink when he gets home from work. It helps him relax."

"Dad's not— Oh, never mind," Victoria said, giving up. She knew the truth, even if her mother refused to see it. It was a lot of drinks, every night, and it was ruining Victoria's life.

Twelve

Luke walked out of the bathroom, a blue terry-cloth towel wrapped around his waist. Better hurry, he thought. He only had about ten minutes to get ready before Nikki picked him up to take a study break. They were going to get some dessert and coffee at the Athenian, a twenty-four-hour diner just outside of town.

Only I haven't done any studying yet, Luke reflected as he headed down the short hall to his room. He'd stayed late at the Tunesmith to help Rick unload a big shipment—he needed all the overtime he could get. Besides, he figured the more effort he put in at work, the less likely Rick would suspect him when the cash register came up short.

He dressed quickly, combed his fingers through his hair, and walked out to the living room, where his mother was lounging on the couch, watching TV. "Mom, it's a nice evening. Why don't you go outside, take a walk?" Luke said. "Or you could read a book or something. You've been in front of the tube like that all day."

Marie Martinson adjusted the red wool afghan that was draped over her body. "This is all I feel like doing."

"But this is the third day in a row you haven't moved from that spot," Luke said. "You can't just sit there for the rest of your life."

"So I'm being a couch potato this week. I need to rest," his mother replied.

"You're not a couch potato, Mom—you're depressed, you're unemployed, and you have to do something about it," Luke pleaded. He felt as if he were talking to a child instead of his own mother.

"Oh, and I suppose you think I can get another job just like that." Mrs. Martinson snapped her fingers. "Maybe you haven't noticed, Luke, but there aren't a lot of jobs around right now for someone like me."

"Sure, if you're going to get drunk on your lunch hour and call in sick because you're on a three-day binge, no, not a lot of employers are looking for a person like that," Luke said bitterly.

His mother didn't say anything. She picked up the remote and changed channels on the TV.

"Mom, listen to me." Luke stood in front of the TV and turned it off. "You've got to pull it together—I can't support both of us! If you don't get a job, we're going to lose this crummy apartment, and then what? Do you want to look for a job while you're homeless?"

"That's not going to happen. Get out of my way," Mrs. Martinson said. "I'm trying to watch—"

"Not until you tell me that tomorrow morning you're getting up, taking a shower, changing into some nice clothes, and going out to find another job," Luke said. "And I don't care what it is. You can find something, Mom. And maybe you'll keep it for once."

"Where do you get off, preaching to me like that? You're no better than I am," his mother said.

"Maybe not," Luke said, "but I don't drink and stay out all night like you. I try to do things responsibly. And I don't make your life miserable, the way you're making mine." But inside he felt a sinking feeling of guilt. *She's right. I'm stealing from my boss.*

"Can I help it if I'm depressed?" his mother cried. "You don't understand!"

"You think I've never been depressed? Are

you blind, Mom? Stupid question—you don't notice anything when it comes to me," Luke snapped.

"No? I notice that you've got a very rich girlfriend and you think you're better than I am," Mrs. Martinson said.

"That's not true," Luke said. "Mom, you need help. Maybe if you saw a therapist, you wouldn't feel like you had to get bombed all the time and destroy yourself."

"Oh, and when did you get your psychiatrist's degree? Did I miss that, too?" Mrs. Martinson sneered.

"No, but you've missed everything else, Mom," Luke said, grabbing his jacket from the back of a kitchen chair. Then he opened the door and ran downstairs. His heart was beating so fast, he had to stop for a second to catch his breath. He and his mother hadn't argued like that in a long time, but he couldn't take it anymore. If she wanted to ruin her life, that was her business. But he didn't want to sit around and watch her do it.

Nikki pulled up in her yellow Jeep about a minute later. "Hey," Luke said as he got in. He leaned over and kissed her lightly on the cheek.

"Hey yourself. What's wrong?" Nikki asked. "Trouble at home?"

"How could you tell?"

"You have this look, like you're really upset only you're pretending everything's normal," Nikki said, taking her hand off the gearshift to touch his fingers.

"My mom's out of control, Nik. She's been sitting on the couch—no, lying on the couch—for seventy-two hours straight. She won't get a job, she won't even move," Luke complained.

"At least she's not drinking," Nikki said.

"Not yet. That comes next in her neat little cycle of self-destruction. Believe me, she's got it down to a science." Luke shook his head. "Never mind. Let's just try to forget about her. About everything." He leaned in closer and ran his hand along Nikki's cheek.

"You know what? The Athenian can wait." Nikki shut off the car's engine and turned to him. She kissed him lightly at first, and then, as he returned her kiss, more passionately.

Now he knew why he needed Nikki so badly. She put up with his moods. She never judged him—or his mother.

And Nikki's kisses made him forget all of his problems.

Two hundred and ten, two hundred and twenty . . . Keith fanned the bills in his hand as he strolled up the walk in front of his house. Talk about a great night, he thought as he stuffed the money into his jeans pocket.

He'd brought only fifty dollars to gamble with because he was afraid that Luke might turn out to be right and his winning streak would come to an end.

Fat chance. He'd picked up thirty bucks on the first hand and never looked back. Sure, he hadn't won every game, but he was smart enough not to bet much money on his bad hands. He could tell that everyone at Mr. Martin's had been dying for him to slip up, to make a false move. There had even been one moment near the end of the night when he had to draw three cards, and he could see everyone's eyes light up when he only matched the high bet instead of raising it.

Then he'd laid down his cards. "Full house," he said, grinning at everyone.

"Why didn't you raise?" Mr. Lopez had asked, looking bewildered.

Keith hadn't answered as he pulled the pile of cash toward him. Did they really think they could guess his every move?

Keith was just about to pull out his keys when he heard the clicking of bicycle gears. Peering down the street, he saw a figure riding toward him, and when it got closer, he saw under the light coming from the streetlamps that it was Katia, with a backpack on her back.

"Hey, what are you doing out?" he asked as

he met her on the driveway. "Isn't it past your curfew—like a full hour past?"

"I was with John," Katia said breezily. "Not that it's any of your business."

"Actually, it is," Keith said. "I'm still your big brother, you know."

"Like I could forget. Look, Keith, you already told me how you feel about me and John dating," Katia said. "You've made it perfectly clear that you don't approve, but that's too bad. You're going to have to get used to it. Everyone else has."

"Including Mom and Dad?" Keith asked.

"Look, Keith, we were just studying, okay? Please don't tell Mom and Dad," Katia begged. "I told them I was studying for a test with some friends, which isn't exactly a lie. They said I could stay out an extra hour. You're not going to tell on me, are you?"

"Of course not," Keith said, opening the garage door for her. "I might not like how much time you're spending with John, but I'd never rat on you."

"Thanks," Katia said, leaning her bike against the garage wall. "I owe you one. Where were you, anyway?"

"With some very good friends of mine, winning every single hand I stayed in on," Keith said. "But you won't tell Mom and Dad about that, either, right?"

"Of course not," Katia said as they walked into the kitchen. "Not yet, anyway."

"What does that mean?" Keith asked, opening the refrigerator. He leaned on the door and stared at her.

"Just don't push your luck, that's all," Katia said.

"I won't." Keith grabbed the container of orange juice from the top shelf. "What makes you say that?"

"These guys you're hanging around with, playing cards with . . . who *are* they, anyway?" Katia asked.

Keith shrugged and poured a glass of juice. "Just a bunch of guys I met."

"Well, just be careful," Katia said.

"Likewise," Keith muttered under his breath as Katia went upstairs to her room. He had a feeling she could get in more trouble with John than he ever could playing poker. A lot more.

Thirteen

"It is *so* great to have an afternoon off from the gym," Suzanne said. It was Thursday, and school had let out for the day. Nikki had invited Suzanne to go for a walk up to Pequot State Park.

"Yeah. I'm glad you could come up here with me," Nikki said. "Luke's at work, Victoria's shopping, Deb's studying for a test tomorrow . . . it seemed like a good chance for us to just hang out by ourselves. Besides, I wanted to show you this spot. It's like my own secret place."

"It's really beautiful and sheltered here," Suzanne said, perching on a rock. "I was afraid you might not want to come here anymore after . . . you know. What happened last weekend."

Nikki sat down, her back against the trunk of a pine tree. "Actually, the accident made it more special to me. It's strange, but I feel like nothing bad can happen to me here."

"Yeah. I understand," Suzanne said, sitting on the ground next to Nikki. She reached into the pocket of her jacket and pulled out a foil-wrapped package. She unwrapped the low-fat brownies and held them out to Nikki. "If there's one thing my mom's good at, it's baking healthy stuff that still tastes good."

"She ought to open a bakery," Nikki said, taking a bite of a brownie. "But I guess she already has her own business."

"Yeah," Suzanne said. "And it keeps her so busy, she's almost never home. She loves it, but it hasn't always been what she wanted to do."

"How's that?" Nikki asked.

"She wanted to be an actress when she was younger," Suzanne said with a sigh. "She even went to Hollywood and tried to make it. But then—" Suzanne stopped. This wasn't easy to talk about, but she knew she could trust Nikki. They were best friends, after all. "She met my father, got pregnant, and had to hightail it back to Brooklyn so her parents could help take care of me."

"Can you imagine something like that happening to us?" Nikki asked.

"No," Suzanne said, laughing. "Definitely not! Not right now, anyway."

"I'm serious. Imagine if you thought your life was going to be one way and you had all these plans . . . and then it turned into something completely different. Not worse—just one hundred and eighty degrees opposite."

"I don't know if I could handle it," Suzanne said. "I mean, I have things I want to do, and I'm going to do them, no matter what. Like acting on Broadway—or off-Broadway. Or off-off-Broadway. Just something, anything, involving acting. Maybe a miniseries . . ."

"Yeah, I'd like to do that, too," Nikki said. "Or maybe be in the movies. I can't wait for the winter play—it'll be way cool if we're both in it."

"First Hillcrest, then Broadway. I hear lots of big stars started out that way," Suzanne joked, and Nikki laughed. "You know, if you wanted to get into TV or movies, you've got all the connections. You've got it made, actually."

"I can get my foot in the door, at least," Nikki admitted. "After that my parents can't help me. If I can't act, I won't get the roles."

"We should take an acting workshop together this summer," Suzanne said. "They've got tons of them in the city. It would be great—we could take the train down in the morning, go to our class, then hang out, meet up with some of my friends later . . ."

"That sounds great," Nikki said. "Too bad we have to wait till June to do it."

"Yeah. That's a long way off," Suzanne said, disappointed.

"Well, my mother always says it's important to start your career early," Nikki said. "So we really should make plans now, like where we want to go to college. We need to pick schools with good theater programs."

"Did your mother major in theater?" Suzanne asked.

"No, journalism," Nikki said. "She got her break when she was an intern at a TV station out in California. One of the news reporters called in sick, and she had to fill in at the last second. She did such a great job, they hired her as an anchor, and the rest is history."

"Wow. Talk about luck," Suzanne said.

"Yeah, well, she had connections, too. My grandfather—her dad—used to own a big production studio in Hollywood, so her name didn't hurt her. Did I ever tell you that my last name is her maiden name? When she and my dad got married, she didn't want to change her name, so he changed his."

"Why didn't they just hyphenate?" Suzanne asked with a laugh. "Or hadn't anyone heard of that way back in the Middle Ages?"

"I guess my dad figured that using her name would help him," Nikki said. "And it did."

"Wait a second—how could the name Stewart help anybody?" Suzanne asked. "It's such an average name!"

Nikki laughed. "Yeah, but my grandfather was a Steven, too—so his company was Steven Stewart Studios. When my dad changed his name, *voilà*—instant celebrity. Name recognition and connections really matter in Hollywood."

"Inbreeding," Suzanne said with a wry smile. "Nepotism. The usual."

"Right," Nikki said.

"So your mother was the one who was successful, and then your father made it because of her—and your grandfather, too, of course. She must be really proud of what she's done—for herself, and for her family."

"She is. But it's also caused problems. There were some tough years when they were younger, when she was a star and he was a nobody. That's what my grandfather told me. They used to fight about it a lot—he wanted her to get him some jobs and she wouldn't, stuff like that."

"So how did they work it all out?" Suzanne asked.

"I'm not sure they ever did, really," Nikki said sadly. "But my grandfather stepped in and gave him a start. Then my father began directing and producing some TV specials and movies, and eventually he got successful in his own right. But they still argue a lot. Actually, my parents can get into it pretty intensely," she added. "They had a huge fight last night."

"About what?" Suzanne asked. Then she noticed that Nikki was on the verge of tears. "I'm sorry. I don't mean to pry."

Nikki shook her head. "No, it's okay. I don't know what they were arguing about, but it seems like whatever it was, it was pretty serious. I still feel lucky compared to other people, though. Everyone's been having such a rotten time with their parents lately," she explained.

"Like who?" Suzanne asked. "Besides me and my mother, that is."

"Well, I don't know if he told you anything about it, but . . . Luke's mother is an absolute mess. She can't hold a job, she drinks and gets really depressed, and then he's the one who suffers. You should have seen him last night. He was so upset because of her."

Suzanne nodded. "That must be rough."

"And Victoria's father can be a real loser," Nikki continued.

"Really? But I thought he was so good to her, buying her all that stuff . . . I guess that's only half the story."

"He drinks way too much, and then he's really weird to be around," Nikki said.

"So is getting drunk and messing up your kid's life a pastime here in Hillcrest, or what?" Suzanne asked.

Nikki shrugged. "I don't know. Sometimes it sure seems that way."

"Well, after hearing that stuff, maybe I should be glad I don't know who my father is," Suzanne said.

"No, don't say that!" Nikki exclaimed. "Don't ever say that. You can't assume anything about him."

"If you heard some of the things my mother said about him . . . He does sound like a real jerk," Suzanne said. "I'd never admit this to Victoria, but maybe my mom was right to give up looking for him."

"Still, there are always two sides to every story, right?" Nikki argued. "What if it didn't happen exactly the way your mom said it did? You know how it is when your friends break up. The guy says one thing, the girl says it happened some other way. You can never tell what really happened."

"That's true." Suzanne smiled. "But the way things are going, Nikki, I don't know what to believe."

"Hey, let's go down to the river," Nikki suggested. "Sometimes just hearing the water is enough to make me calm down and feel better about everything. It always works . . . except, of course, the last time I tried it."

"Are you sure you want to?" Suzanne asked.

"I guess it's like getting back up on a horse that threw you," Nikki told her. "I have to face the fear. You know, all that self-help junk."

The two of them stood up and walked the hundred yards or so to the river's edge. Listening to the water rush over the rocks and watching it cascade down the hill in the waterfall, Suzanne could hardly believe she'd had the nerve to jump into it less than a week earlier.

Not that she would change anything, she thought, glancing at Nikki out of the corner of her eye. And if Nikki did fall in a second time, she'd jump right in there after her all over again.

John walked into the locker room after practice on Thursday and tossed his helmet onto the floor outside his locker. If there was one thing he couldn't stand, it was a lousy practice. He'd barely connected on any passes, and he'd been intercepted twice and sacked once. He could still hear Coach Kostro yelling at him. "Badillo, you call that a pass? Come on, guys—get serious! Don't you want to win?" If the team didn't pull it together soon, they weren't going to have another winning season like the previous year's, and John knew that as the quarterback, he would end up getting most of the blame.

Keith came into the locker room and sank down onto a bench. "Man, I'm exhausted."

"I don't know why," John said. "You didn't put anything into practice."

"What do you mean? I was running for the past hour and a half straight," Keith replied.

"Yeah, right. Maybe you were running, but you sure weren't *thinking*. Not about football, anyway. You looked like a zombie out there, just like everyone else. If this team doesn't get it together, we can forget about the state championships," John complained.

"The opening game's still a week away," Keith said. "Why are you talking about the state championships already? We'll pull it together when the season starts. Don't worry."

"I'm not the one who should be worried, buddy boy. You are. You dropped three passes in a row, Keith. Keep that up and I'll find another receiver to throw to," John threatened.

"You can't do that," Keith said. "We're a team. We've got all the patterns down. If we do as well as we did last season, we'll be in the Hillcrest record books for life. Not to mention all those college scouts who'll be checking us out."

"That's what I'm telling you," John said. "You've got to shape up. If you don't get it together and stop thinking about three-of-a-kinds, straight flushes, and whatever else is on your mind, you're not getting a college football scholarship to anywhere."

"You're telling *me* to concentrate?" Keith tossed his shoulder pads onto a bench. "That's a good one. You were so busy checking out the cheerleading squad, I'm surprised you could even keep the plays straight."

"I was not!" John yelled.

"Come on, man. I saw you staring at them," Keith said.

"So maybe I was watching a cheer or two," John admitted sheepishly. "What's wrong with that?"

"What's wrong with that?" Keith took a step closer to John. "You're supposed to be dating my little sister, or have you forgotten since last night, when she came sneaking home past curfew?"

"I haven't forgotten anything," John said. "Besides, she said she only ran into you because you were coming home from another night of gambling. If I were you, I'd be more worried about my gambling than about my sister's love life. What's your problem, anyway?"

"I just don't want to see you treat Katia the

same way you treated Laurie, and Susan, and Monica, and—"

"That's ancient history," John said. "It's got nothing to do with what's going on now between me and Katia."

"No?" Keith asked. "Well, it'd better not. That's all I'm saying."

"For your information, I'm serious about Katia," John said. "Probably more serious than I've ever been about any girl."

"Even Victoria?" Keith asked.

"Yeah, even Victoria," John said. "So don't worry about me and what I've done before. I'm not going to mess this up, and I'm not going to hurt Katia."

"You sound pretty sure of yourself for someone with a lousy track record," Keith said.

"It's called growing up," John said. "Look into it, dude."

"If you're so concerned about growing up, then why don't you date someone your own age?" Keith shot back. "Instead of taking advantage of someone who's innocent, who's never dated anyone before, who's only a sophomore—"

"Your sister's not ten years old anymore," John said. "She can look out for herself. Anyway, you don't need to worry. I'm taking it slow, Keith."

"You'd better," Keith warned.

"What, are you threatening me?" John said. "Keith, it's her life. If she wants to date me, she will."

"Just don't hurt her," Keith said. "Don't break her heart. That's all I'm saying."

"And I'm telling you, I won't," John insisted.

Fourteen

"So, Ian, are you going to Nikki's party tonight?" Victoria casually slid into a seat opposite Ian in the cafeteria.

Ian nodded. "Yeah, I think so. Sounds like everyone will be there."

"Everyone who's anyone, anyway," Victoria said, gazing around the cafeteria.

"Actually, I hope more people than that show up," Ian said. "Otherwise it's going to be pretty boring."

Victoria gave him a quizzical look. "Are you saying you want everyone at school to be there? Is that what you mean?"

"The more the merrier, right? That's what my dad always says," Ian said. "Kind of dorky, I know, but that's Dad. He's from Generation Dork."

Victoria laughed. So Ian did have a sense of humor. "Hey, speaking of your dad, is he still dating Suzanne's mom?" she asked.

"Yeah, I think so," Ian said. "Not that my father talks much about it."

"Oh, of course not," Victoria said. "That would be tacky. I was just wondering if maybe he and Ms. Willis had talked about Suzanne's father." Maybe she'd be in luck and Ian would have some new dirt on Suzanne.

Ian shrugged. "I wouldn't know. I don't listen in on my father's private conversations."

Too bad, Victoria thought, tapping her nails against the table. Sometimes that's the only way to find out anything.

"Well, I guess I'll see you tonight," she said, standing up. She didn't want to wear out her welcome. Maybe if Ian got a glimpse of what he was passing up by not paying attention to her, he'd wake up. Then again, maybe not, she thought as she looked at him. He was already back to reading the computer magazine on the table in front of him.

"Good-bye, Ian," she said.

"See you," he mumbled without looking up.

Why do I even bother? Victoria wondered as she walked away.

But she knew why.

She'd always been obsessed with guys who played hard to get. It was usually too easy for her to get a guy's attention, so naturally she was more interested in those who resisted her at first. Of course, if Ian didn't budge in her direction soon, she'd give up altogether—she didn't feel like spending the rest of her life trying to win him over.

On her way out of the cafeteria, she passed by John and Katia. Katia was sitting on John's lap, and the two of them were so intertwined they looked like a giant pretzel.

Victoria felt a pang of jealousy, but pushed it away. She'd gotten used to seeing John with other girls, though never somebody he seemed so serious about. John had moved on with his life—why couldn't she?

Well, maybe my love life isn't as exciting as his, but I do have plans to improve it. They're just not working, that's all.

But if Ian still wasn't interested, she was sure she could find somebody else. She wasn't about to spend her entire senior year all alone.

"I love pineapple on pizza," Deb said as she and Suzanne sat down at a table at Pizza Haven in Hillcrest Plaza on Friday afternoon.

"No offense to Pizza Haven or the state of Connecticut, but this pizza really isn't New York style, the way they advertise on their sign."

"Yeah, but the important thing is, it's hot,"

Deb said. "I can't believe how cold it's gotten outside already. Between yesterday and today it's, like, a thirty-degree change. No more Indian summer."

"I guess not," Suzanne said. Then she sighed with contentment. "I can't believe it—two days in a row I don't have to go work in Mom's studio. I'm feeling spoiled. And, speaking of spoiled, did you see that bracelet Victoria's dad gave her?"

Deb nodded. "It's awesome. I wish someone loved me enough to get me something that expensive."

"It doesn't always work that way, you know. I mean, sometimes people give you expensive stuff just because they feel guilty about something, not because they love you."

"Yeah, well, I don't have much luck in the love department anyway," Deb said. "Haven't you heard Victoria calling me 'Sweet Sixteen and Never Been Kissed'? I'm getting so sick of it. I think I'll slug her the next time she does it." Deb threw a couple of quick punches in the air.

Suzanne knew she was kidding. Deb was just about the nicest person she'd ever met. She couldn't imagine the pretty, petite girl fighting with anyone. "Okay, you may not have had a serious boyfriend, but isn't there someone you're interested in?"

"There's always someone I'm interested in," Deb said with a laugh. "The problem is, they're never interested in me."

"So who is he?" Suzanne asked in a whisper, leaning closer to the table.

"Actually, I think Ian Houghton's really cute. But that's typical of me. I pick the same guy that Victoria does. Like he'd even notice me when she's around," Deb complained.

"I don't think he noticed Victoria much on their date last weekend," Suzanne said. "From what I heard, Ian seems more into computers than girls. Maybe you'd better find another guy to drool over."

"The way I feel now, I don't think I'll ever find a guy. It's like with my birth parents. I know they're out there somewhere, but I wonder if I'll ever meet them face-to-face. What about you? Do you think you'll ever meet your father?"

Suzanne thought about the picture of Steven Carew her mother had given her when she was a little girl. In the picture, he had his arm around her mother, and they were both smiling. Suzanne carried that photograph in her wallet—it was wrinkled from all the times she'd taken it out to look at it and wonder about how her life might have been different if her father hadn't died.

Only now she knew that the whole time he'd

been with her mother, he'd been planning to leave her. And their happiness in the photograph was all a lie. Was somebody like that worth finding?

"I don't know, Deb," Suzanne said. "It's easy to have this fantasy about a great reunion and how special it'd be, but what if I do look for my dad and find him, and then it turns out that I hate him? Or what if he doesn't like me? Or what if he has a whole new family and doesn't want me to be part of it?"

Deb shrugged. "I know. I think about the same things. If I do find my birth parents, it might be nothing like the way I want it to be. But I have to know, Suzanne." She sipped her soda. "Sitting around and wondering about it is pure torture. Not knowing where I come from or why they gave me up for adoption—the unanswered questions are worse than anything I could find out."

"I'm sure they had a good reason. Anyway, it's different for you," Suzanne said. "You don't know anything about either one of your biological parents. I grew up with my mother—although lately I've been feeling like I don't know her at all, either."

"Really?" Deb asked.

Suzanne nodded. "Yeah."

"You and your mom will work it out."

"How can you be so optimistic?" Suzanne asked.

Deb shrugged. "What's the alternative? Walk around and think the worst is going to happen all the time? That won't help, and it won't change anything."

"I guess so." Suzanne thought of Luke. Maybe she and Luke were more pessimistic than people like Deb and Nikki because bad things had happened to them, because things hadn't always worked out the way they'd hoped.

Stop obsessing about Luke! she told herself. Suzanne looked at Deb and smiled. "You know what? I'm glad we can talk about all this stuff. But if you really want us to be true friends, you're going to have to promise me one thing."

"What?" Deb asked seriously.

"Promise you won't ever get fruit on your pizza again. It totally grosses me out," Suzanne joked. "How about if we split a slice of old-fashioned pepperoni pizza instead?"

Luke wiped his hands against his faded black jeans when he noticed Rick coming toward him from the back of the store, where his office was. Every time he saw Rick lately, Luke instantly got nervous and sweaty. He barely had time to stuff the money he'd just taken from a customer under the cash drawer, where he'd retrieve it later.

"Hey, Luke," Rick said. "I have a question for you."

"Sure," Luke said. "Shoot."

"Am I crazy, or didn't you just sell a copy of the new Pearl Jam CD about five minutes ago?" Rick asked.

"Um . . . yeah, I think I did," Luke said slowly.

"That's funny. The inventory hasn't changed any," Rick said.

"What do you mean?" Luke asked, panicking.

"I was just running our weekly hot-sellers report, and the numbers don't match up. The computer doesn't show that we've sold any today," Rick said. "I could have sworn I'd seen a couple of people buy it this afternoon."

Luke knew this could be it—the end of his job, and worse. He had to think up an explanation, and he had to think fast. I should tell Rick the truth and get this whole thing over with. I should come clean, tell him how much I've taken, and make a plan to pay it back.

Luke cleared his throat. "You know, I've noticed that before. Sometimes it takes the computer a few minutes to register the numbers."

"Really? I don't remember reading that in the program manual," Rick said.

Luke shrugged. "Maybe it's a bug in the system."

"Hmm. Well, I'm still calling this our top seller, even if the numbers don't reflect that." Rick took a stack of Pearl Jam CDs from a box and started filling a display rack.

As soon as Rick was a safe distance away, Luke grabbed a Pearl Jam CD and punched in the computer code that was on the back of the plastic cover. He rang up three. Then he took the money he'd put aside from underneath the drawer and put it in the register as cash received for the sold CDs. That way the numbers would be more like what they should be.

He wouldn't go home with any extra cash that night, but at least he'd keep his job . . . for the time being, anyway. If Rick was getting suspicious, though, Luke would have to find another way to get the extra money he needed—and soon.

Fifteen

"I can't believe it's still raining," Nikki complained. "Now no one will show up." She, Suzanne, and Deb were standing in her kitchen, putting together some plates of snacks before everyone arrived for the party, which started at seven-thirty.

"Come on—Nikki Stewart, the most popular girl at Hillcrest High, is throwing a party," Suzanne said, stirring onion soup mix into a bowl of sour cream. "Do you seriously think anyone's going to pass that up because of a few drops of water?"

"Don't worry, Nikki. I mean, it's only all everyone at school was talking about today," Deb said.

"You look great tonight, by the way," Suzanne told Deb, who was wearing a cropped red cardigan sweater over a tiny white T-shirt and black jeans. "Red looks really good on you."

"Thanks. You look nice, too," Deb said.

Suzanne smiled. She had practically ransacked her closet, trying to find something to wear that night. She wanted to look hot but not too sexy. The last thing she needed was for Nikki to think she was trying to attract Luke's attention. So she had settled on an oversized turquoise cotton tunic with a deep V-neck in front and in back, and striped leggings.

"So, Deb, maybe tonight's the night you'll find Mr. Right," Suzanne said.

"You mean Dudley Do-Right?" Nikki added, laughing. She opened another bag of pretzels and dumped them into a glass bowl.

"Very funny, you guys." Deb sighed. "Actually, I think his name is Mr. Nonexistent. Don't get your hopes up. I've totally given up on meeting anyone new. I mean, don't we already know everyone at school?"

"Not everyone," Nikki said. "And besides, some people might bring friends who go to other schools."

"Or they might have cousins," Suzanne added. "Come on, Deb—you're the one who's always so optimistic. If you don't think you're going to meet someone, then you won't. It's as simple as that."

"Maybe so, but don't feel like you have to

set me up with anyone," Deb said. "Don't make finding me a date our next group project, okay? If I find someone I like, fine—if I don't, there's no law that says we all have to have boyfriends. I don't see anyone asking Suzanne who she wants to see here tonight."

Luke, Suzanne thought quickly. Then she glanced at Nikki, afraid the other girl could tell what she was thinking. Deb's comment had made her feel incredibly awkward. If she couldn't have Luke, and John was history, who *was* she interested in now? She was going to have to look for someone new. Someone to get my mind off Luke, she thought as she watched Nikki for a reaction. Nikki was busy arranging celery and carrot sticks on a plate and didn't look up.

Suzanne cleared her throat. "That's because you both know I'm not interested in anyone right now. Especially after my dating disaster with John," she lied. She was glad Victoria wasn't there to pounce all over that statement. "So, where's Victoria?" she asked. "Isn't she coming?"

"Oh, there's something you have to know about Victoria," Deb told her. "First of all, she never actually does any work when one of us has a party. Even at her own house, she doesn't lift a finger, except to tell the caterers what they're doing wrong."

"And second, she's really into the concept

of being fashionably late," Nikki said, glancing up at the clock on the kitchen wall. "I wouldn't expect her until at least nine."

"She loves to make a grand entrance. We used to place bets on when she'd show up," Deb said. "Down to the minute. It was a great game, only John always won."

"Yeah, he knew her pretty well. Still does, I guess." Nikki paused. "You know, she hasn't said anything exactly, but I think she's having a hard time dealing with seeing Katia and John together all over the place."

"All over each other is more like it," Deb said.

"That too. But even though Victoria's the one who dumped John, I think she still wishes they were together," Nikki said.

"We didn't exactly hit it off, but I have to admit, he is gorgeous," Suzanne said. "I had a few friends in Brooklyn who weren't half as good-looking, and they were models."

"Yeah. That's the problem. He's so good-looking that not only do girls hit on him all the time, but he thinks he can date anyone on the planet," Nikki said. "He really took Victoria for granted."

Victoria tossed a red strapless dress over her shoulder. Nope. Not that one. She pulled a long, crinkled floral skirt out of the closet.

Last year's news. She stood in the doorway to her closet, staring at the stacks of sweaters and racks of blouses.

She had to find something truly amazing to wear. This was the party that was going to start her school year all over again—okay, maybe it was supposed to be for Suzanne, but Victoria could easily steal the limelight if she wanted to. As if Suzanne was any competition in that department! Of course, she was pretty, and she *was* in incredible shape. . . .

Well, I would be, too, if my mom owned a gym, Victoria thought.

She decided she'd have to go for the delicate look. It was a little cold and rainy out, but Nikki's house would be plenty warm. She took a sheer black short-sleeved blouse out of the closet and tossed it onto her bed. Then she added a silk camisole, a pair of wide-legged patterned black-and-white trousers, and her new black platform shoes.

Casual yet elegant, she thought as she admired herself in the mirror. The fact that the shoes made her about five feet ten didn't hurt. She did her makeup, stuffed a lipstick into her miniature purse, then, seeing that it was still pouring outside her window, took her black trench coat out of the closet and walked downstairs.

"You look like a million dollars, Victoria,"

her father said when she went into the kitchen to pick up her car keys from the hook on the refrigerator and grab an umbrella. "Maybe a couple of million."

"Thanks, Daddy." Victoria slipped her arms into the trench coat. "I'll be at Nikki's house for the rest of the night, okay?"

"The boys are going to be lining up at that party just to get a chance to talk to you."

Victoria arched one eyebrow. "I doubt that."

"Don't be so modest. We Hills are headed for greatness. I've got big plans for this family," Mr. Hill said. "We're moving up, honey."

"Beverly Hills? Palm Springs, maybe?" Victoria had been fantasizing about moving to a new place, one where people might appreciate her a little more.

"No, nothing like that." Mr. Hill chuckled. "Something much closer to home, actually." He dropped an ice cube from the tray on the kitchen counter into his glass, then filled the glass with Scotch. He lifted the drink to his lips and took a long sip.

"Such as?" Victoria prompted, wondering what her father was getting at.

"I've made a decision. I'm going to run for deputy mayor," Mr. Hill said.

"You? But—"

"But nothing. You saw how well I hit it off

with the mayor the other day, didn't you? We've discussed our options, and we think this is the best way to go. We can work together to get the zoning laws changed the way we want, bring in new business to Hillcrest . . ." Mr. Hill took a long drink from his glass.

Victoria cringed. Her father, running for office? If the press started digging for dirt on the candidates, they were going to find out about her father's favorite workout—lifting a glass of Scotch. John was the only one who knew how serious her father's alcoholic bouts and rages were. Sure, everyone knew that he drank, but they didn't know how much, or how often, or what usually happened when he did. Even her own mother wouldn't face the truth about how much Victoria's father really drank.

"So whaddaya think?" her father slurred.

Victoria could just imagine the stares she'd get from everyone when she walked into school after her father's name was plastered all over the morning paper. And the condescending things people would say, the pity in their eyes. No, she couldn't stand that.

"Whaddaya think of your old man becoming a politician?" Mr. Hill repeated. "First deputy mayor of Hillcrest, then governor of the state, and maybe one day I'll—"

"I think you're getting carried away," Victoria said.

"I'm just joking. I only want to stay in politics long enough to get that luxury mall built over by the park," Mr. Hill said. "It's wasted space."

As much as Victoria liked to shop, she wasn't sure she agreed that the space was being wasted. It was such a pretty drive up to Pequot State Park—what were they going to do, build a mall right up against the side of the mountain? But she was in no mood to argue with her father at the moment. She had a party to go to.

"Well, Daddy, I have to run, or else all the boys are going to be taken by the time I show up," Victoria said, picking her purse up off the counter.

"Not a chance." Mr. Hill smiled at her. "But 'fore you go, I have to know—you do support me, don't you, Victoria? It's very important to have my family behind me. The press would have a field day if my own family wasn't one hundred percent behind me, you know?"

"Daddy, I'd vote for you if I could, and as long as you put all my favorite stores in that luxury mall, I don't care what you do," Victoria said. "Good night."

"Try to stay dry, and have a good time." Mr. Hill opened the front door. He was a little unsteady on his feet.

Try to stay dry. I ought to give him the

same advice, Victoria thought on her way out the door. "Oh, I'll have a great time," she told him, glancing at her watch. Ian would be at the party by now—just in time to catch her dramatic entrance.

And this time he would notice her. She was going to make sure of that.

Sixteen

"I told you this was going to be a great party." Nikki strained to be heard over the loud dance music coming out of the stereo speakers. "This place is packed!"

Suzanne looked around the crowded living room at everyone dancing, talking, and yelling to each other. There were colored helium balloons sticking to the ceiling, and Nikki had draped a banner over the fireplace mantel that read "Thanks, Suzanne!"—which embarrassed Suzanne a little.

Nikki's parents had bought enough food to feed a small army: besides the appetizers she, Nikki, and Deb had prepared, there were pizzas that had just been delivered, as well as a six-foot-long submarine sandwich, and coolers filled with every kind of soda imaginable were stashed all over the house. Suzanne had never been to a party with so much of everything.

"So how do your parents feel about huge crowds?" Suzanne asked.

"They're okay with it. Actually, they're hanging around, just to make sure things don't get out of control," Nikki said. "It's happened before, believe me. One time a bunch of older guys crashed a party here, and they were really bad news. They stole some stuff and spilled beer on my mom's favorite Oriental rug. After that, my father said he'd make sure he was here whenever I had a party. He thought about getting private security, if you can believe that. That's what Victoria's parents do when she has parties."

"Probably a good idea," Suzanne said.

"Hey, Nikki, great party!" Sally Ross was moving to the music as she approached the snacks table near where Suzanne and Nikki were standing. "I love guacamole," Sally said, dipping a tortilla chip into the bowl.

"Well, if I have any leftovers, I'll let you know," Nikki said with a laugh as Sally headed back to the dance floor.

"Hey, you guys, how's it going?" Keith walked up to them, holding a big sub sandwich in one hand and a cupcake in the other.

"Sure you've got enough to eat there?" Suzanne asked.

"For the next fifteen minutes, anyway," Keith said. "Hey, Nikki, where's Luke?"

"He's not here yet. I'm getting a little worried, actually," Nikki said.

"Don't. He'll be here," Keith said.

"Why aren't you guys dancing?" Deb asked, coming over to them as a song ended. She wiped her forehead with a napkin.

"We're waiting for a great song," Suzanne said.

"When it happens, will you dance with me?" Keith asked.

"Sure," Suzanne said. "Thanks."

"You don't have to thank me. I mean, who wouldn't want to dance with the guest of honor?" Keith asked. "I'm hoping I'll get my picture in the paper, actually."

"Oh, I see how it is," Suzanne replied. "You're in it for the publicity factor."

"There's Luke," Deb said, pointing behind Suzanne. "Hey, there's Victoria, too. I guess the party has officially started now."

Suzanne's smile vanished as she glanced over at the entrance to the large, sunken living room. Luke and Victoria were talking, heading toward them. Luke looked extremely cool and laid-back in an old gray gas station jacket over a white T-shirt and black jeans, while Victoria was dressed for another, fancier party, as usual. Suzanne started to smile at Luke, but then stopped. She couldn't act too nice—but she couldn't totally ignore him, either. She had no idea how to act around him now.

"I'm going outside to get some fresh air," Suzanne said quickly. "It's getting stuffy in here with everyone dancing."

"Hello! Earth to Suzanne." Nikki waved her hand in front of Suzanne's face. "It's pouring out there. You'll get soaked."

"Oh, right," Suzanne sighed. "I forgot." She'd have to find another excuse to wander off. But before she could think of one, Luke was standing in front of her.

He took Nikki's hand and kissed her quickly on the lips. "Sorry I'm late," he said. "This weather is the worst."

"Hey, nobody's allowed to be in a bad mood at my party," Nikki told him, wrapping her arm around his waist.

Suzanne felt a twinge of pain, seeing them so close together, watching as Luke's lips touched Nikki's. She'd avoided them as much as possible all week, because she was still struggling with the fact that she had lost Luke . . . and that he apparently hadn't had any second thoughts about giving her up.

"Sorry. I had a bad day at work," Luke said.

"Why? What happened?" Deb asked.

"Nothing, really. It was just one of those annoying retail days, that's all."

"Tell me about it," Deb said. "Remember how long I lasted at that cute dress shop downtown?"

"How long was that? One and a half hours, or was it two and a half?" Victoria teased her.

"Hey, I was there two whole months," Deb said.

"Well, all I know is that you didn't stay there long enough for me to get your discount on the spring line," Victoria complained.

Deb shook her head. "I keep forgetting that my purpose in life is to make sure you get the right clothes. You look great, by the way."

"Yeah, Deb's right," Suzanne said. "I love your outfit. It's very hip."

"It's okay. I'm not thrilled with it," Victoria said.

"Way to take a compliment," Keith told her.

"Maybe we should take a trip into New York next weekend and do some real shopping," Victoria said.

"That's a great idea," Suzanne said. "Nikki and I were just talking the other day about a trip to Manhattan," she explained to Victoria.

"Well, don't let *me* get in the way," Victoria huffed, and she walked off across the room to talk to somebody else.

Suzanne looked at Deb and shrugged. She watched out of the corner of her eye as Luke and Nikki wandered off to a corner of the room by themselves. He hadn't even acknowledged Suzanne, hadn't even said hello.

"I think I'll go mingle," she told Deb. She just wanted to be alone for a minute and not have to look at Nikki and Luke in envy. Suzanne made her way down the hall and stopped at an open door. The den, where everyone had stashed their wet coats and umbrellas, was completely empty for the moment.

Suzanne walked in and slowly worked her way around the room. There were the awards on the mantelpiece for Nikki's mother's TV show, and on one wall were photographs of Nikki as a baby, as a young girl, as she was now, with her parents . . . and there was a picture of her with Luke.

She stopped in front of the desk, staring at a framed photograph of a young Nikki standing on a ship's deck with her father. They had their arms around each other, and they were smiling for the camera as if they didn't have a care in the world. Suzanne couldn't help envying all that Nikki had: her nice, neat life with both a mother and a father, all the money she could ever want or need, and, of course, Luke . . .

She kept staring at the picture. Something about Nikki's father's smile . . . it was familiar, somehow. Almost as if she'd recognized it from a long time ago. But that was ridiculous—she'd only known Mr. Stewart for a few weeks.

No, she was sure she knew that man. And she suddenly realized where she had seen him before. Suzanne ran to the pile of coats and desperately grabbed her bag. She reached in and found the photo she always carried with her. Slowly, her hands slightly shaking, she held it up against the picture.

"What?" she mumbled. "But this—it's impossible!" It was an exact match. It was him.

Her father . . . and Nikki's father . . . it was the same man!

Suzanne turned away from the photograph, her blood pounding in her ears. She was having a hard time catching her breath. She had to stay in control, to make sense of what this all meant to her.

A plaque on the wall caught her eye. "In recognition of ten years of devoted service to the United Way. Steven C. Stewart."

Steven C. Stewart . . .

She recalled what Nikki had said about her father having taken her mother's name when they got married. So . . . the *C* could stand for Carew. But that was crazy. He couldn't be her father. Maybe he just looked a lot like him.

Then again, Suzanne's mother had said Steven Carew was a producer, that she'd met him in Hollywood, and that he'd lived in San

Francisco. That was where the Stewarts had lived until Mrs. Stewart moved her TV show to New York.

It was all beginning to fit together. How her mother had come up with the money to move out of Brooklyn and open her own workout studio. How they'd been able to buy a house. Why it was all happening in Hillcrest, Connecticut, a town Suzanne had never even heard of a few months back.

"A silent partner," her mother had said. That silent partner was more than a business partner—he was her father!

That was why he'd hugged her so tightly at the hospital the day she'd saved Nikki, and why he and her mother had given each other such strange looks, as though they knew each other from a long time ago. They certainly did!

"It's funny how alike we are about so many things," Nikki had said the other day on their way back home from Pequot State Park. "Almost like we're related."

"Separated at birth," Suzanne had joked. Some joke. Nikki and I are half sisters! Did Mrs. Stewart know, too? Did everyone know except her? But there was no way Nikki could know. How would she react when she found out?

Suzanne's stomach tightened into a knot,

and she grabbed the back of the desk chair to steady herself. Her mother had lied to her more than she could ever have believed possible. All of her pathetic lies echoed in Suzanne's head: "He doesn't know about you." "I haven't seen him since then." "I didn't even know he was still alive."

For all Suzanne knew, her mother and Mr. Stewart had been having an affair ever since they'd moved to town—or else why *had* they moved to Hillcrest? Certainly not so she could get to know him, since they obviously hadn't planned on telling her about any of this! Her very own parents had tricked her, lied to her.

Her entire life was one big lie!

Suzanne panicked when she heard footsteps behind her. She couldn't face anyone and pretend she was just another teenager at a party. As she turned around she realized she was still clutching the framed photo.

"Suzanne?" a deep male voice said.

Hearing Mr. Stewart's voice made Suzanne shake all over. He wasn't Mr. Stewart anymore—he was Dad, though Suzanne was sure she could never call him that, not ever.

"Why aren't you out there with the rest of the gang?"

Mr. Stewart was standing in the doorway, smiling at her. She couldn't stop thinking of him as Mr. Stewart, even though she now knew he was Steven Carew.

Suzanne wasn't prepared for the wave of hatred she felt toward him. She wanted to run at him, punch him and kick him as hard as she could. But she was so stunned, she couldn't speak or move. She felt as if she were in the middle of a horrible nightmare.

"Suzanne? Is something wrong?" His voice was filled with concern. "Are you all right?"

A tear rolled down her cheek, followed by another, and then another. "You," she finally managed to choke out. She held the crumpled photo toward him. "You're—him! You're Steven Carew!"

Mr. Stewart turned pale. "Suzanne, I can explain—"

"Don't explain anything!" Suzanne cried. "Just tell me if I'm right!"

He nodded. "Please, I—"

Suzanne threw the framed photograph onto the hardwood floor. The glass smashed into a hundred pieces and scattered across the room. Then she ripped the photo she was holding in two, tossed the jagged halves in her father's face, and ran out of the room.

Nikki was just coming out of the bathroom as Suzanne ran past her toward the front door.

"Suzanne, where are you going? What's wrong?" Nikki tried to grab her arm, but

Suzanne threw her hand off, practically shoving Nikki against the wall.

That's your half sister, she told herself as she ran outside into the pouring rain. You have a sister and a father, right here in Hillcrest.

But at the moment, running down the Stewarts' driveway, with rain streaming down her face and mingling with her angry, bewildered tears, Suzanne felt as if she had nobody in the world at all.

And she didn't know where she was running to, either, because she had nowhere to go. No one to talk to. She had only a lying mother, who'd conspired with her father to keep her real identity a secret—and the two of them had kept this from her for her whole life! It was too awful.

Between the rain and her tears, Suzanne couldn't see where she was going. She tripped over a large rock at the edge of the Stewarts' driveway and went flying to the ground, landing face first on the rough gravel. Suzanne didn't even care. She just sobbed harder. Things couldn't get any worse.

Seventeen

"So, Ian, how about if you and I go out tomorrow night? Only this time, let's do something that doesn't involve a computer. I can think of a few things that are much more interesting." Victoria gave him her sexiest look as she ran her finger over his hand. Now all he had to do was pull her into his lap and—

"Yeah, maybe," Ian said, moving his hand away.

Victoria felt like throwing her glass of club soda in his face. Hard to get was one thing, but it was absolutely impossible even to have a decent conversation with Ian. Any guy in the world would jump at the chance to go out with her—any guy except Ian Houghton!

She'd had enough of this dumb party, anyway. With one last look at Ian, Victoria left to say good-bye to everyone. She was looking around for Nikki in the kitchen when John came over to her.

"Hey, can you do me a huge favor?" John asked.

Victoria shrugged. "Sure. What is it?"

"Would you give Katia a ride home?" John asked. "Keith left a little while ago, and she has an eleven o'clock curfew to make. I'd take her, but I'm supposed to give Luke a ride—he had to take a cab over here—and I can't find him anywhere."

Victoria sighed and glanced at her watch. What a wasted evening. First Ian, now this. John hadn't even asked her to dance once at the party. And now she was only worth talking to because she had a car? Why had she even bothered getting dressed up? No one had noticed her. Not even John, who was, as usual, looking beyond gorgeous. *If only I hadn't broken up with him*, she thought regretfully, *I'd be the one in his arms instead of Katia.*

Then she had an idea. She could drop Katia at her house, then rush back to the party and hang out with John. If anyone could make her feel better, it was John. They'd sit together, reminisce about the good old days when they were a couple, and maybe, just maybe, have a little fling for old times' sake.

No, she thought, looking around the party

and seeing Katia laughing and talking to Deb. Maybe Suzanne Willis is low enough to steal somebody else's boyfriend, but I'm not. John and Katia were happy together—she wouldn't come between them. She liked both of them too much to do anything so underhanded. Besides, part of her knew that even if she made a play for John, he wouldn't be interested. He cared about Katia now. Not her.

"Sure, no problem," she told John with a sigh. "But tell her that I want to leave right away. I'm not having the best time in the world." She stared at the "Thanks, Suzanne!" banner hanging above the Stewarts' fireplace.

Yeah. Thanks, Suzanne. Thanks a lot, Victoria thought as she walked to the den to get her stuff. Thanks for coming to Hillcrest and taking my best friend away. She stepped carefully over shards of broken glass on the floor. It looked as though somebody had been having a good time. She wondered who could possibly have made such a mess. She picked up a few of the biggest pieces and put them on the desk, beside the torn picture she found on the floor.

Funny—I've never seen this photo before, she thought. It looks like Mr. Stewart and another woman. Maybe it's his sister. She picked up her trench coat and walked to the front door, where she waited for Katia.

"Victoria, you're a total lifesaver," Katia said as she rushed over and joined her at the door. "If I miss curfew, I'm grounded for a week."

"No problem," Victoria said. "Let's just go, okay?"

"See you guys later." John kissed Katia, and Victoria turned away as the kiss turned into a make-out session. Asking her to give Katia a ride was fine and all, but did he have to rub in the fact that they were ecstatically happy? It was so frustrating, she felt like screaming. Nothing she did was working out right. And if she ever got a date again with somebody who was as nice as John, she'd be surprised. She was stuck with the Ian Houghtons of the world, guys who paid more attention to inanimate objects than they did to her.

Victoria opened the door, and raindrops immediately pelted her face. "Just my luck," she muttered. She was leaving the party in the middle of a monsoon.

"It's pouring," Katia said.

"Here, you take my umbrella, and I'll make a run for it." Victoria held the top part of her trench coat over her head and dashed toward the car. She unlocked the car doors as quickly as she could and ducked inside. "Great—now I'm totally soaked on top of everything else," she muttered.

"I'm really sorry about this," Katia said, closing the door, her wet raincoat and the umbrella dripping all over the leather seat.

"Don't be silly. It's not your fault it's raining," Victoria told Katia. Still, I deserve better than this, she thought. Way better.

Victoria slowly backed the car out of the driveway.

"If only Keith weren't being such a flake lately, I wouldn't have to ask," Katia went on. "He's been out the past two nights at some stupid poker game. He's making a ton of money, only he has to sneak around, and he can't spend any of it because my parents would get suspicious."

"Mmm." Victoria was only half listening to Katia. She turned right and headed down the road toward the Steins' house. It was at least two miles out of her way, and all she wanted was to get home, go up to her room, and then soak in the tub for an hour, until she forgot what a rotten night she'd had.

"You should hear him, Victoria. He thinks he's the best card player on earth," Katia said. "Just because he's been winning lately. Actually, you know what I told him today? I told him if his ego got any bigger, he'd have to sleep on the lawn tonight, because his head wouldn't fit through the door." Katia laughed softly.

she knew she'd adjust to it eventually. It didn't have anything to do with Katia. "But let me give you a piece of advice. Be careful."

"Why is everyone saying that?" Katia complained. "First Keith, now you. I may not be as old or experienced as you guys, but I can look out for myself."

"I'm not saying you can't," Victoria said. "I'd give the same advice to anyone dating John, that's all."

"Maybe things are different between us. Oh, never mind. I don't want to argue with you. I just didn't want there to be any tension between us, that's all."

"Likewise," Victoria said, looking at the right side of the road as an oncoming car neglected to dim its brights.

"So what are these other problems you've been having?" Katia asked. "Anything I can do to help?"

"I don't need any help, from you or anybody else," Victoria snapped. Now, on top of everything else, she had little Katia Stein feeling sorry for her and wanting to help with her love life? She pressed her foot harder against the accelerator as the road straightened. The sooner she dropped off Katia, the better. The nerve of John, asking her to drive his new girlfriend home. She would have a couple of things to say to him the next time she saw him. Such as, I think you have me confused with someone else—a chauffeur.

"Sorry. I just thought— Hey, do you see that car? It's weaving in and out up there," Katia said nervously. "Maybe you'd better pull over."

"What car?" Victoria said, irritated.

"Coming toward us," Katia gasped. "See it?"

Victoria had just enough time to see an oncoming car's headlights veering back and forth as the car drifted from its lane into Victoria's. Suddenly the car was heading right at them!

"Victoria, pull over!" Katia screamed.

The car was headed diagonally across their lane. At the last second Victoria pulled the steering wheel to the left as hard as she could to get out of the way. She heard Katia scream in terror.

We're going to die! Victoria thought fleetingly. And then she couldn't think anything, because her car was slammed backward down the road, the passenger side smashed, the windshield shattering and metal crunching. And Katia's awful, horrible scream had suddenly ended.

Victoria came to with her forehead pressed against the padded steering wheel. She sat up slowly, her head reeling with dizziness. The windshield was shattered, and small pieces of glass were sprinkled all over her lap and in her hair. They were even clinging to her hands, which still gripped the steering wheel.

But she was okay, she realized, feeling her face for cuts. She winced as she pressed on her right cheekbone. It felt swollen already. "I'm going to look great tomorrow," she said, turning to Katia, her voice wobbling. Her nerves were completely shot.

Victoria felt her heart leap in panic when she saw Katia slumped forward, motionless. She gasped as she saw that the side of the car had crumpled around Katia, so that the passenger-side door was pressed up against her.

"Katia?" Victoria reached out and touched her friend's arm. When Katia didn't answer, Victoria shook her arm gently. "Katia, wake up! Come on!" But Katia's arm was limp, lifeless. She wasn't responding at all.

Victoria unfastened her seat belt and moved in her seat so she could get a better look at Katia. "Come on, Katia. Talk to me," she pleaded. She reached over and touched Katia's hair, then slowly lifted her chin up so she could see her face. Katia's eyes were closed, and blood was trickling out of the corner of her mouth.

Oh, my God. Victoria leaned across Katia to see her other side, closer to the door where the car had been hit. She almost gagged.

Katia's shoulder was practically twisted out of its socket.

Victoria knew she ought to check Katia's pulse, but she couldn't bear the thought that she might not have one. All she knew was that they needed an ambulance, fast. She'd have to flag down the first car that passed. Katia was bleeding and unconscious, and she had to get help.

Her heart pounding, Victoria gently leaned Katia's head back against the headrest and opened her own door. Her legs were shaking so much, she could barely stand up. When she got out of the car, though, she saw another car idling on the shoulder. Through the pouring rain, she could just barely make out the shape of the vehicle that had run them off the road. It was a Jaguar.

She took a step toward the car, hoping the driver would have a cellular phone, and hoping, despite her anger at the driver for causing the accident, that nobody else was hurt as badly as Katia.

But before she could get close, the Jaguar backed up—fast! The wheels spun, throwing out mud, then the driver pulled onto the road.

"Stupid drunk driver!" she yelled. Victoria couldn't believe that somebody could run her car off the road and then drive away, as if nothing had happened, when she was standing there screaming for help, when her friend might be dying!

The car turned one hundred and eighty degrees so that it was headed back in the direction it had come. It was briefly illuminated by the headlights from Victoria's own car, and she got a better look at it.

A red Jaguar.

Could it be . . . ?

Then she glimpsed the vanity license plate, and all doubts were erased from her mind in an awful realization.

Katia was hurt, maybe even dead. And it was all her father's fault.

About the Author

Jennifer Baker is the author of two dozen young adult and middle grade novels. She is also the producer for TV Guide Online's teen area and teaches creative writing workshops for elementary and junior high school students. She lives in New York City with her husband and son.

Printed in the United States
By Bookmasters